Jenny's Justice

ROMANCING THE SPIRIT NOVELLA SERIES

CB SAMET

Romancing the Spirit

cbsamet.com

Cover Design by: Get Covers

eBook ISBN: 978-1-950942-21-3

Print ISBN: 978-1-950942-20-6

A ROMANCING THE
SPIRIT NOVELLA

JENNY'S JUSTICE

CB SAMET

One

"Why do you want to ruin a good thing?" he demanded.

A wave of rage surged inside him. How dare Cecilia try to blackmail him? Did she comprehend who he was?

He tried to reason with her, but the conversation escalated to arguing, followed by threatening. They had a mutually beneficial relationship. He'd paid for her time and expertise. Now she was pulling this stunt?

They argued in her living room, a minuscule space with a small, flickering television and a couch that reeked of cheap perfume. He struggled to keep his voice low. No one could know he was there. He wouldn't have stepped foot into this dump if she hadn't turned against him.

"Everybody gets mad. But everybody pays." Her pupils were pinpoint, tiny little beads swimming in a sea of blue fire.

No wonder she was being so brazen. She was high on drugs. She'd told him her routine once: amphetamines in the morning, cocaine in the afternoon, sedatives when she needed sleep.

She knew how to regulate the drugs she gave herself, and nights with her intoxicated made for a fun time. But this drug addict thought she could get away with black-mailing him? Not in his lifetime.

"Drop it," he snapped, the force of his words driving her backward into the kitchen, another cramped room with bland white cabinets and cheap laminate countertops.

"I'm not paying you a penny. You think you'll ruin me? I'll ruin you." He poked a firm finger at her.

"What're you gonna do?" Cecilia scoffed. "Send me to jail for drug charges? Been there, done that. I'll be out in a less than a month. I don't have anything to lose. You, on the other hand, have a career, a house—well, a couple of them —and probably wife number three in the pipeline. You have a lot to lose, so don't try to go head-to-head with me." She poked a long acrylic nail into his chest with each of the last several words.

Panic flared as fury saturated every crevice of his mind. He did have a great deal to lose. He couldn't let her get away with this. On primal instinct, before he understood his own actions, his hand closed around the handle of one of her kitchen knives.

And then there was blood. So much blood.

JENNY SAT at the prosecutor's table watching the jury follow the defense attorney's every move.

He walked gracefully in his shimmering slate suit and

spoke in a deep, authoritative voice, smooth as liquid satin while he began his opening statement. Like a fine, expensive bourbon with a burn so smooth you actually enjoyed it. "My name is Beaufort Montrose, but people call me Beau. Now, South Carolinians pronounce Beaufort as *Bew-fert*. Here in North Carolina, we say *Bo-fert*. To keep it simple, call me Beau."

Calm and congenial.

Jenny suppressed an eye-roll. If she had a golden coin for every time she had to hear Beau Montrose talk about his name, she'd have a collection to rival her father's. And yet, the jury always melted into an adoring puddle at Beau's feet. Some combination of his impeccable hair, captivating blue eyes, confident stroll, and melodic voice lured them to his side. Of course, as the prosecuting attorney, she was immune to his charm—at least she wanted to be.

Song of the Siren

She scratched the words into her notebook with her black ballpoint pen. The scent of the fresh ink wafted toward her.

What did she have to combat Beau's glamor? Her suit was from a mall department store and never seemed crisp despite careful ironing. Her thick blonde hair was pulled back into a bun—because who had time for anything else? At least her bangs were even. Mostly. Her name certainly didn't have a movie star ring like Beaufort Montrose.

The smitten jury tracked Beau's every movement as they sat in black high-backed chairs behind a half wall of polished mahogany. To their left, the wooden pews were packed with spectators.

"Now, Miss Jenny Wiley here will try to convince you my client has broken the law," Beau continued eloquently. "But I ask you to carefully focus on the facts and the facts only. Be careful not to confuse established facts with loose conjecture."

Truth, Jenny reminded herself. She had truth on her side. She reached into her pocket and rubbed the coin she carried as she glanced at the defendant.

Guilty.

She had the truth. The defendant had pulled the trigger and killed his employer. When Jenny walked the jury through events as they'd unfolded leading up to the murder, they would see the truth. No high-priced defense attorney—not even the best in Charlotte—could hide Bubba Hollins' guilt.

Work your magic, Beau. It's all smoke and mirrors.

BEAU MONTROSE CAUGHT sight of the assistant district attorney leaving a judge's chamber.

He quickened his pace to catch up to her. "Fraternizing with the judge," he teased.

Jenny Wiley shot him a look of daggers without slowing her pace. Her heels clicked on the marble flooring. Beau chuckled. She was fun to rile, and her reputation was so squeaky clean that they both knew his words were weightless.

"Nice presentation this morning," he continued in

honest admiration. "Although, you wasted too much breath on a case I'll win."

"Not this time," she said.

He arched an eyebrow. "Such confidence."

Her tone of conviction was one of her tells—like a gambler. Whenever Jenny insisted the defendant was undeniably guilty, Beau's job became an interesting uphill battle. He felt a little giddy at the thought of the challenge ahead.

Jenny Wiley brought his acquittal ratings down, though he was still one of the most sought-after defense attorneys in the city. The damage to his record was mildly irksome but perhaps a needed dose of humility. She posed a challenge—an exciting call to action to stay at the top of his game. And because she was a formidable adversary, a victory against her would be that much sweeter.

He glanced at her apparel. Her charcoal suit fit her slender figure nicely and revealed shapely calves. A faint ginger-orange fragrance wafted off her.

"There's a throng of reporters out there," he mentioned mildly as a warning so she wouldn't be caught off guard.

She hesitated and touched her hair. The bun she'd started the day with had developed rogue fly-away strands, but they only added to her beauty.

"Miss Wiley, I'm not suggesting you look unprepared. On the contrary, you look quite lovely," Beau said.

She frowned. "I don't like reporters."

"Allow me. I'm happy to address them first. See if I can calm them down before you address them."

She eyed him suspiciously as if wondering if he was playing her.

He wasn't manipulating her, but she was free to think

what she liked. His job description was to impress clients with his bold brand and media show, not the DA's office. Some prosecutors disdained his flair, but others understood the purpose of his theatrics. Sadly, Jenny had always unmistakably fallen into the disdain category.

"After you." She gestured.

He gave a polite nod before stepping outside. His smile widened. "If it pleases the press," he said to the crowd of reporters, "I can take just a few questions." He made a show of checking his watch.

All eyes focused on him. The volley of anticipated questions came at him.

"Do you have any evidence to refute the State's case?"

"How will you handle the witnesses who say they saw your client leaving the scene of the crime?"

After grabbing a latte, Jenny returned to her office to work on additional legal notes. Her office was small, but she was one of eighty-five assistant district attorneys, so working space was always a negotiation and a source of contention.

She'd made a solid case against Bubba, but logic and truth didn't always prevail in the courtroom, especially when Beau Montrose was on the opposing team.

Her discontent with him stemmed from simultaneously admiring what an outstanding lawyer he was and disliking his peacock display of strutting around the courtroom. His media antics added to her irritation, but that behavior was exactly what his clients wanted.

"Jenny," a voice greeted her at the door.

She looked up from her paperwork to see Stu Winslow, Charlotte's shining District Attorney, standing in her doorway. Stu wore a gray suit over a white shirt and red tie. His black leather shoes had been polished to a high shine.

Despite his perfectly waved blond hair turning white, his neighborly charm, and easy smile, his presence set Jenny on edge. Stu didn't appear in the doorway of an underling's office unless he wanted something.

"How are you, Stu?" She'd learned the hard way not to ask what she could do for him or why he was there when he spontaneously appeared. If he wanted something from her, she wouldn't make it so easy.

"I'm doing well. I wanted to see how you're faring after your opening remarks on such a high-profile case."

He'd been hovering incessantly ever since she'd been assigned lead on the Bubba Hollins case. She supposed the trial of the son of a congressman who'd supported Stu's election made him nervous. Because she wasn't an elected official, she had no problem throwing her full capabilities into the case to convict a murderer. Stu had voiced his concerns about her being junior, even though she was part of the Homicide Team of prosecutors. She'd argued that her track-record indicated she was ready.

When he hadn't backed her a hundred percent, she'd refrained from reminding Stu of the many other cases she'd helped him prepare. When his success had been in some part due to her efforts, she'd received no credit for her impact.

But that was okay; she was biding her time. All of the effort was part of office politics. She scratched his back; he'd scratch hers. When the time came for promotion or larger cases, more prominent cases, Stu would remember how she'd been a team player. He would remember, wouldn't he?

Reaching into her jacket pocket, she rubbed the coin, feeling the textured surface. "I've got wisdom, justice, courage, and temperance on my side. I'll be just fine." She had evidence also, but that didn't guarantee a win.

"That's good, because I watched Beau Montrose putting on a display at the press conference, and I didn't see you countering—reassuring the community that the killer would remain behind bars."

"I assure you, the killer will remain behind bars. I gave my statement after Beau. The media chose not to air it."

Stu smiled, somehow wide but not friendly. "Okay. These career-making cases are tricky things. They can also be career-ending."

With that edgy, veiled threat, he turned and left.

Beau observed Jenny's closing arguments with interest. Her summation was precise, emphasizing key points in the trial without regurgitating every detail to a saturated jury. She appealed to their analytical reasoning rather than their emotion. Without straying from the facts, she kept her arguments concise.

The courtroom was heavy with intense focus. He loved the ambience of the arena with its presiding judge on a throne of mahogany, cove of jurors, and array of spectators adding tension and drama. All of this encapsulated in room filled with a long history of life-altering decisions.

Beau had represented his client as best he could, letting the burden of proof fall squarely on the prosecutor. He'd raised credibility issues with witnesses, where applicable, and argued against small timetable discrepancies that existed.

But the prosecution had a solid case, and Bubba Hollins had been unwilling to plead guilty.

Jenny spoke with a soft voice, yet still commanded the room. She and Beau had been on opposing sides for several years now as he built up his practice in Charlotte, but he knew very little about her personally outside of work.

That probably wasn't going to change. Jenny was a straight arrow, no nonsense, no fraternizing with the enemy type of person. And Beau preferred not to entangle himself in the kind of drama that would inevitably follow if he pursued the whimsical idea of getting to know an assistant DA.

When the session was adjourned to allow the jury to deliberate, Beau stepped into the hallway and checked his phone.

Five missed calls and three text messages.

He debated for a moment whether to respond now or take a few minutes to see if his client needed reassurance before the final verdict was released. Bubba had been mostly rude, arrogant, demanding, and demeaning throughout the trial. Beau had enough self-worth that Bubba's behavior didn't bother him. He also understood that his clients were under a great deal of stress and their behavior wasn't always reflective of their true personality. However, he didn't think that assessment applied to Bubba Hollins.

With that in mind, Beau opted not to play the role of consolatory hand-holder and listened to his voicemail instead.

He stepped into a corner near the window to avoid the crowd awaiting the jury's verdict.

"Beau, this is Karl." His cousin's voice sounded edgy and distraught. "This is my one phone call, man. I need your help. I'm in jail. Cecilia is dead, and they think I murdered her."

Two

Jenny pulled a beer from the tin bucket on the table and twisted the top off.

"Congratulations!" Mary, one of her work colleagues, raised her glass in a toast.

"Thank you."

Jenny and several colleagues had gathered at *Howl at the Moon* in downtown Charlotte for an informal celebration. About thirty people from the office had come to the bar to bask in a big win for the DA's office. But collegial outings were tricky. Jealousy and office politics were always factors, and she had to be careful about the role she played, which meant modest acceptance of praise and no over-consumption of alcohol.

Although she had a plethora of colleagues, she didn't connect with them on a personal level enough to consider anyone a friend. Some saw her as competition, others as a conquest. Some were jealous, others indifferent. The few most similar in personality to her were also too deep in their careers to make time to socialize.

She wished her dad was alive to see her victory—her big win. He would be proud, and she could have been herself around him and enjoyed her success. Reflexively, she placed her hand in her suit coat pocket and touched her father's coin.

Bill, another colleague, slung an arm over her shoulder. "Hey, gorgeous. Congrats on the win." His whisky sour sloshed in his glass, nearly spilling on her.

"Thanks, Bill." She eased out of his embrace, fairly sure he was less interested in her win and mostly wanted to sleep with her.

Guilty, came the reply from the coin she still touched.

"I have some ideas about how we can celebrate," Bill said with a wink.

She didn't actually need the coin to tell her the man's intentions, but having instant access to the truth made dating in general a challenge. Although she tried not to use the coin regularly outside the courtroom, she wasn't trusting by nature.

"No, thanks, Bill. It's been a long week, and I plan to relax alone."

After she wriggled away from him and through the crowd, she made her rounds to greet everyone.

Mary clinked bottles with her again. "Head-to-head with the gorgeous Beau Montrose. You've got nerves of steel to keep your wits about you around that man, am I right?"

Jenny took a swig of beer. "He's something, all right." He was attractive, single, and impossibly full of himself, judging by his courtroom tactics. But Jenny was proud of her win because he was a formidable defense attorney, not because she wasn't distracted by his good looks and smooth voice.

A half hour later, when the crowd was several drinks into the night, Jenny quietly left, ready to relax in the comfort of her apartment.

THE NEXT DAY, Jenny sank into her desk chair. After months of preparation, days of courtroom presentations, and her win in the Bubba case, she should have felt elated and energized.

Instead, she was utterly drained. As she lit a small stick of orange ginger incense in a crystal vase on the edge of her desk, she looked disparagingly around her office. She needed to tidy the place up, especially organize loose papers, file folders, and discard sticky notes. But what she wanted to do was dissolve into a hot bath with a glass of buttery Chardonnay before crawling into bed to watch *Alias* reruns.

As the incense burned, she breathed in the soothing fragrance and closed her eyes. Leaning back in her chair, she took a moment to recharge.

"Victor's remorse?"

Jenny jerked upright to see Beaufort Montrose standing in her doorway. Her initial annoyance had her envisioning leaping over the desk and high-kicking him Jennifer Garner style, not that she had any of the TV character's prowess.

When Jenny saw Beau's disarming smile, the *Alias* fantasy flipped upside down and mingled with her bathtub imagery, and suddenly, he was drinking Chardonnay with her.

She cleared her throat and pushed to her feet. "Never," she replied.

His amused smile widened, crinkling the edges of his eyes. "Good for you. Congratulations on a well-deserved win."

The sincere note in his voice disoriented her, causing a mix of elation and wariness to shoot through her.

"Why are you here?" Shouldn't he be writing his next speech for his on-camera performance, soaking up the limelight and waxing poetic to the press about how his client was actually innocent and the courts would discover this in appeals?

"I can't congratulate you as a colleague?" he asked, blinking at her innocently.

She didn't like the way her eyes roved his tall figure lurking in her doorway. She wanted to shove him out of it and refused to acknowledge the part of her that whispered *tell him to step inside*.

To her astonishment, he walked into her small, cluttered space. Filled with his presence, the temperature of the room seemed to rise.

"You're the only ADA I rarely win against. And when I do, it's because the details of the case aren't airtight."

"Um, thanks?" She narrowed her eyes at him.

He continued, "You have a special selection technique when you pick your cases. Almost like you know who's guilty."

Her hand reflexively went to her side—toward the

pocket where her father's coin rested, but she had taken her jacket off and laid it over the chair earlier.

"Maybe you just choose to represent the guilty ones," she challenged.

"Everybody deserves representation." He straightened her name plate on her desk, and for a moment her eyes fixated on his large hands and long fingers. They were more rugged and less manicured than she'd expected.

"You sleep well at night knowing criminals walk the streets because of you?" she asked. She believed in representation for all, but she wouldn't allow someone as showy as Beau to receive anything but polite disdain.

"Win or lose, I go to bed every night knowing I did my best and held the prosecution to a high standard. Yes, I sleep very well."

Ugh. Now she was envisioning him nestled between the sheets with hair tousled and eyes half-lidded.

He added, "Blackstone's ratio: *'for the law holds that it is better that ten guilty persons escape than that one innocent suffer.'* Of course, Ben Franklin suggested one hundred persons rather than just ten."

"Can I help you with something, Mr. Montrose?" As soon as the rhetorical question escaped her lips, she wished she could reclaim it. There was nothing in this world she wanted to help him with except exiting her imagination.

A wolfish smile lit his face. "Yes, you can. I'm representing a new client, and he looks quite guilty."

"Shouldn't be a problem for your conscience."

"Not at all." He shrugged. "But I'd like you to meet him and give me your impression."

"You want me to meet your client?" She crossed her arms.

"Yes. You're not the prosecutor, so there shouldn't be a conflict of interest."

She scrubbed her hands over her face. "I don't have time for this."

"Sure you do." He pointed at her with a light gesture. "You just won a big case. You can rub my nose in it on the way to the county jail."

She pursed her lips.

He shifted his weight—his classic courtroom tell that he was about to change tactics. "Tell you what. If you meet him now, I'll spring for golf tomorrow. Quail Hollow."

"You want to play golf with me?" She moved her name plate back to crooked just to show him he had no right to touch her things.

"If you win, I won't bother you about my new client ever again."

She strummed her fingers on the edge of her desk. She'd never played an elite course like Quail Hollow. "I like that wager."

He beamed. "Excellent. Now, come meet my man. And if you still feel like I wasted your time, I'll buy you Greek takeout."

"Greek?" As if on cue, her stomach rumbled at the prospect of her favorite food. How did he know?

She plucked her suit jacket off the back of the chair and followed Beau out of her office.

BEAU AND JENNY walked down East Trade Street toward the Mecklenburg County Detention Center, passing attorney and bail bonds offices. Her practical heels clicked on the concrete sidewalk. The hot sun beat down on them, but fortunately, the distance outside was mercifully short.

He was relieved the assistant DA agreed to visit the county jail with him. He genuinely was worried about his ability to clear Karl Dixon's name.

Beau wanted to get Jenny's perspective on the accused, but he also wanted to see how she worked. She didn't view every charged suspect as a criminal. She had a selection process to whom she assigned guilt, and her intuition was better than par. He wanted to know how she consistently outplayed the competition.

Although pleasant in appearance with silky blonde hair and a trim brown suit, Jenny was such an introverted, absent-minded professor type. Her courtroom notes were chicken scratch on a legal pad. Her office was a mess of disorganized papers. She even had one of those old-fashioned typewriters. Who used a typewriter in this century? With such a haphazard workplace, it was a miracle she ever won a case.

Still, she had a clever knack for painting clean, concise pictures for the judge and jury. And she even occasionally managed new evidence to condemn the accused before the trial concluded. So, while her life was a poorly maintained community golf course full of hazards, her legal cases were a clean, manicured Augusta National.

This made Jenny a puzzle. Beau liked puzzles, but not complicated women. Was she complicated? Messy, yes, but maybe not so complicated. After all, in the span of five minutes, he'd won her over with a golf invitation and a meal. In preparation for winning Jenny to his side—at least long enough for her to meet his client—he'd discovered her favorite type of food through one of her work colleagues with whom he'd played golf.

"What are the charges?" Jenny asked as they walked side-by-side.

"Murder."

She gave a dry, humorless chuckle. "Of course it is. Beau Montrose doesn't do dull."

"Life's too short for dull," he said.

This time she genuinely laughed, and he was surprised to learn he liked the sound. For just a moment she wasn't irritated with him for bribing her with sports and food or irritated with herself for acquiescing.

"That's funny?" he asked, smiling.

"It just seems like something you'd say. I happen to like some very dull moments interspersed in life."

"Oh?"

"The courtroom is enough drama. At the end of the day, I like a nice, dull evening of relaxation and stress relief."

"Stress relief doesn't have to be dull," he said.

She shot him an incredulous look with heat in her cheeks. He hadn't intended to flirt with her, but he enjoyed the response enough to do it again when the opportunity presented itself.

"How far into the case are you?" she asked.

Back to business. Was this because she wasn't interested in him, didn't date the opposition, or had a boyfriend? And why was he curious?

"He's been arraigned. I should receive the police reports Monday for review."

"Why do you doubt your client's innocence? What are the circumstances?" she asked.

"He was found over the body, murder weapon in hand."

"Seriously?" She stopped abruptly to gape at him.

"He says he found her that way." Beau put a hand on her elbow to keep Jenny walking. He didn't want to stand in the North Carolina late spring humidity in a suit one minute longer than he had to.

"Next, you'll tell me he was covered in the victim's blood."

"Well, yes, he was." Beau smiled at her exasperation.

Jenny shook her head before glancing up at the large, white concrete building that was the Mecklenburg County Detention Center.

Upon entering the jail, they showed identification to the clerk and signed the roster.

Jenny turned to Beau again before they entered the holding room of the accused. "You want me to meet this person and give you my impression? You realize I'm biased already from the picture you painted."

He nodded. "That works in my favor if you walk out of that room thinking he's innocent."

STU DABBED his mouth with a napkin after a bite of his sesame seared tuna at *The Capital Grille* off Tyron Street. Around him, lunchtime conversation mixed with the clinking of silverware and the ice in tall glasses of water and sweetened iced tea.

Across the two-seater table from Stu sat Congressman Hollins wearing a sour expression and barely touching his food.

"My son was convicted of murder, Stu. That wasn't supposed to happen."

"Your son is guilty of murder, Congressman Hollins. I can't work miracles. My underlings are a tenacious group of self-righteous, naïve, truth-seekers. They are exactly the type of lawyers they're supposed to be in the DA's office. They aren't going to throw a case any more than a dog willingly surrenders his bone."

Stu rubbed his palm against his napkin, but the red stain on his hand didn't wipe away. He hid his hand beneath the white tablecloth.

The congressman irritably turned his fork on the table. Bags hung under his dark eyes, but he still maintained a tidy appearance with trim gray hair and a custom suit. "I thought if we hired the best defense attorney, combined with our working relationship, we could make this go away."

"I can't work miracles," Stu repeated. "You'll take it to the appeals court. The drama of the trial will have died down by then, and Mr. Montrose will be in a better position to use his charm to win the appeal. The murder was simply too fresh in the minds of the jury."

Stu didn't like the defense attorney, but he grudgingly had to admit that Beaufort Montrose was excellent at his job and had perfect showmanship.

"That's the best you can do? I supported your campaign," the congressman reminded him.

Stu had made a name for himself as a tobacco defense attorney before campaigning for DA. He had higher political ambitions, and angering a congressman wouldn't work in his favor.

"And I appreciate that. And that's why I've given you inside information during the ongoing trial of your son." Stu shifted his weight in the chair and lowered his voice. "Look. I obviously have a few friends in the police department who don't mind helping with extracurricular activities for a price. Perhaps new evidence regarding your son's case can come to light in time for the appeal. Or old evidence could be tainted." Politics required tough decisions.

The congressman gave him an appraising look. "I can't get reelected with my son in prison for murder."

Stu turned the stem of his wine glass in a slow circle where it rested. The red liquid swirled thickly, looking unnervingly like blood. He opted not to take a sip.

"Do you love your son, Congressman?"

Hollins grunted and looked away. "Not this year."

Stu tapped a finger gently on the table. "The simplest route may be to have something tragic happen to him in prison. Whatever you decide, I'm sure we can help each other."

Three

At the door to the holding room, Jenny hesitated. A shimmering form stood beside a man seated at the lone table under fluorescent ceiling lights. This ghost of a woman wore skin-tight short-shorts, a halter top with enough cleavage to hide a sand trap, and outlandishly styled black hair framing her face.

Jenny's mouth went dry and her heart thudded wildly as she struggled to keep her composure. Her father had warned her this might happen. The ghost anchored to the coin he'd given her was only a voice damning the guilty, but someday he'd said she might see actual ghosts.

Why now? Why in front of Beau Montrose of all people?

The accused sat at the table, fidgeting nervously with his cuffs. He had a triangular build with broad shoulders and trim brown hair. He wore a standard county jail orange jumpsuit.

With the walls still tilting on her, Jenny took a deep breath, steeled herself, and entered the conference room.

Beau followed behind her.

"Karl, this is Jenny Wiley, the lawyer I told you about," Beau introduced them. "She'll ask questions, and they may seem redundant. I know you've been over this with the police and with me, but we'll review it again with Miss Wiley."

Jenny took the seat at the table, avoiding eye contact with the woman beside Karl. So far, the ghost acted as if she knew she was a ghost, unseen by everyone in the room. She smacked gum, picked at her fingernails, and didn't try to address anyone nor appear to expect an introduction.

"Mr. Dixon, can you tell me about the night of the murder?" Jenny asked.

Hollow eyes stared back at her. From guilt or despair, Jenny couldn't determine.

"I went over to my sister's apartment. We were supposed to hang out and watch movies—brother and sister Friday night." He took a shaky breath.

"What does your sister look like?"

"Pretty. Dark brunette. Cecilia—CeeCee—didn't need to wear makeup, but she always did, you know, for the job. She had blue eyes like mine. And she liked wearing this ridiculous fake mole." He gave a humorless chuckle.

Jenny glanced up at the woman who touched a hand to the mole on her face and shot her brother a disparaging look.

"She was an escort?" Jenny asked.

Karl glanced at Beau, obviously assuming he'd shared that bit of information with Jenny. If Beau was surprised at her "deduction," he didn't show it.

"What happened at your sister's place?" Jenny asked.

Karl wrung his hands together. "The door was closed. I let myself in and found her on the floor ... with a knife." He let out a half-choking, half-sobbing noise. "With a knife sticking out of her chest. I called for an ambulance."

"Was the door locked or unlocked?" Jenny asked.

"Unlocked. I remember thinking that was weird because she always locked her door. Then I thought maybe she unlocked it knowing I was coming over for a visit."

"What did you do after you called 9-1-1?"

"My paramedic training kicked in. I checked her pulse and didn't feel one. She wasn't ... lividity hadn't set in yet, so I figured I should do CPR. But I can't do CPR with the *freaking* knife sticking out of her chest. You're not supposed to remove impaled objects, but I didn't have a choice. I took it out and started chest compressions. I mixed it up with mouth to mouth. One-person rescuer. Two breaths and thirty compressions."

Cecilia the ghost sniffed as she listened to her brother's story.

Karl's voice cracked. "They think I did this. They think I could do this to my own sister."

Leaning back in her chair, Jenny sized up Karl. She liked to reach her own conclusion before touching the coin. If his was an act, it was a good one. But he could be both anguished about his sister's death and the responsible party. There was only one way to know for sure. She reached into her pocket and grasped the medallion.

Innocent.

Goosebumps trailed down her arms. She pulled her hand out of her pocket and left the coin in its resting place.

"Why are the police sure you did it?" she asked.

"Because I'm convenient. They can close the case and go back to eating doughnuts if they pin it on me."

"Motive?"

Beau placed a hand on Jenny's shoulder. "There's an inheritance to be gained. Therefore, money was a motive."

What's the story of this inheritance?" she asked, acutely aware of Beau's touch, but appreciating how it helped ground her as she interviewed Karl with his sister's ghost in attendance.

"Our parents set up a trust," Karl said. "We each receive a certain amount of payments starting at age twenty-five until we reach thirty-five when we receive the balance in a lump sum. CeeCee burned through her funds pretty quickly. She had substance abuse problems and was in and out of rehab. Expensive rehab. A more fiscally responsible person could've lived comfortably off the inheritance." He scrubbed his hands across his face a bit awkwardly. "She liked nice things."

Karl wiped at his eyes before continuing. "In Latin, Cecilia means blind. She was blind to the destruction she caused in her own life. She used to get so mad at me when I'd tell her that."

Cecilia shook out her hands as she spoke for the first time since Jenny entered the room. "Oh, Karl. I'd like to tell you I'm sorry, but I'm the dead one in this situation. They're going to pin it on you because it's convenient and because nobody will believe it was an elected official."

Jenny cleared her throat to stifle her surprise at Cecilia's words—words only Jenny could hear. Resisting the urge to speak directly to the ghost, Jenny force her gaze on Karl.

"Did Cecilia have any enemies?" Jenny asked, invoking

all her willpower not to make eye contact with the apparition in the room.

Karl snorted. "She knew dirt on everybody she associated with in her business. I wouldn't be surprised if she was blackmailing half the men she slept with. But she didn't share any secrets with me."

Secrets.

The woman had numerous secrets which may have culminated in her murder. And if Cecilia had taken those secrets with her to the grave, Jenny would have to actually talk to the ghost to learn the truth. That terrifying thought had her vision blurring and heart racing.

Jenny simultaneously did and did not want to know the ghost's terrible secret of who killed her. She always sought the truth, but if it was an elected official, finding the truth —and proving it—could be a risky undertaking.

"You think he's innocent." Beau felt a pep in his step as he kept pace beside Jenny's fast stride after they left the jail.

"Maybe. Dang it. Yes." As she walked, color pinked her cheeks.

Beau preferred the rose hue to how pale she'd looked walking into the conference room at the jail. Something had spooked Jenny back there, but she'd kept her composure and finished the interview.

"What's the rush? Is there a fire somewhere I don't know about?" he asked.

"I need to get home." Her voice was a little breathless.

"What makes you think Karl is innocent?"

"I don't want to discuss it right now."

"Okay. Do you want to talk about what's upset you?" Beau asked.

"No." She didn't slow until she reached the parking garage, and she hadn't made eye contact with him since the interview.

Beau had never seen Jenny so distraught. Through all their court time together in opposition, she was cool under pressure. This flustered side of her was different, and he felt unnerved that he might've done something to cause it.

Then again, maybe she had meltdowns on Friday afternoons and this was normal behavior for her. She obviously wanted space; he needed to give it to her, but backing off wasn't one of his strengths.

"Jenny." He tugged gently at her elbow before she could push open the stairwell door. "Did I do something to upset you?"

She stared at him, wide-eyed, as if caught off guard by his concern. Biting her lip, she glanced nervously around as if someone might be following them. When she shook her head, she pulled her arm away from him.

"No, you didn't," she said.

"I owe you dinner." Maybe he could coax out what troubled her over a meal. She'd been genuinely interested in his offer for Greek cuisine only an hour ago.

"I'll take a raincheck."

He frowned.

She pursed her lips. "Golf tomorrow, right?"

"Eight a.m. tee time."

"I'll see you then."

When she vanished into the parking lot stairwell, he was left to wonder what troubled her, and why the heck he wanted so badly to know.

~

WHEN JENNY ARRIVED at her apartment, she called her sister, Phoenix, and told her she'd won the Bubba Hollins case. She'd arrived home too late last night after the celebration to phone.

"I know! I saw the news. I'm so proud of you! I wish I could be with you to celebrate."

"Thanks." Jenny dropped her keys on the counter of her apartment and began opening a bottle of wine.

"Um. You do not sound appropriately stoked."

"I have a big problem. I saw a ghost today." She tugged out the cork and set it aside.

"Oh? Related to Dad's coin, or something else?"

"An actual murder victim," Jenny said.

"That's not creepy at all."

"Have you seen one yet?" Jenny poured the cabernet into a wine glass.

Phoenix had told Jenny she'd thought she'd seen ghosts once or twice in passing, but she hadn't claimed to have seen any in a few years.

"No. Well, maybe. I'm hearing music," Phoenix said.

"You work on Broadway," Jenny pointed out. Her sister performed on-stage in New York.

"Yeah, thanks for that. But this is solo singing backstage when I'm alone. Beautiful, mesmerizing music."

"Like *Phantom of the Opera*? And you haven't seen an actual ghost?"

"No. Just that intoxicating male voice."

"You're giving me goosebumps. Let me know if you ever see him." Jenny breathed in the wine before taking a sip.

"If I ever do, it would be hard to have a romantic relationship with a ghost. Anyway, what are you going do about *your* ghost?" Phoenix asked.

Jenny knew this day would come. Her father had warned her. In fact, she'd expected it sooner in life. She'd heard whispers and voices sometimes. Cool breezes or warm gusts of air had brushed over her in places where there were no open windows or no ventilation. But a real, whole, fully-interactive ghost was a new experience for her.

She swirled the wine in her glass as she considered Phoenix's question. "It's complicated because I'll have to ask the victim who killed her, and I think she knows. Then, I'll have to try to prove the murderer committed the crime without seeming insane. I'm not an investigator. I do not investigate. Not ever. And I can't exactly claim that my source was the murder victim herself."

"Anonymous tip? Don't the police get those all the time?"

"It might work to lead the police to evidence, but it won't work to name the culprit that way. I have to have real evidence."

And she would have to find it alone. As far as she knew, no one she worked with could see ghosts. She had friends in the police department, but they wouldn't help her in Karl's case without a compelling reason. And she couldn't tell them the reason was that the victim's ghost identified the killer. She would lose all credibility in this case and every future interaction with law enforcement.

Investigating a murder was outside her jurisdiction and training. Venturing into unknown territory alone was a recipe for failure. Yet, Karl and Cecilia were depending on her.

~

BEAU ARRIVED HOME THAT NIGHT, still baffled by Jenny's behavior but determined to have a pleasant and relaxing weekend.

He entered the kitchen and pulled out the ingredients from the refrigerator to make stir fry.

"Hey, Dad. How was work? I saw you lost the Bubba case." Travis entered the kitchen and opened the drawer to pull out the wok. He was a tall, lanky sixteen-year-old with dark hair, a little longer than Beau would've liked, and his mother's eyes.

"Can't win 'em all." He shrugged, rinsing the vegetables.

"Did you see Karl today? How's he holding up?"

Travis liked to keep up with Beau's cases in the news, but in this instance, he'd been following the local news because he'd once met Karl at a family reunion.

"As best he can under the circumstances." Beau chopped broccoli first, followed by the zucchini.

Travis got the canned baby corn and water chestnuts out of the pantry.

"I've got golf tomorrow. You've got lawn mowing and basketball?"

"Yeah." He twisted the can opener. "How can you go play golf with what's going on with Karl?"

Beau stopped chopping. This was an excellent time to discuss the importance of compartmentalization. "I'm going to help Karl, but I don't even have police reports yet to review. If I deprive myself of enjoyment every time a client is suffering, I'd have none at all. If you want to be a doctor, you're going to have to learn how to compartmentalize also." He resumed chopping vegetables.

"Doesn't that make a person callous?"

"Compartmentalizing doesn't make you callous. It keeps your mental and emotional health in check. If you fall apart when the job gets tough, you're no use to anyone."

Beau was determined to not only be useful to Karl, but to clear his name of murder. Yet clever words and charm wouldn't save Karl if the evidence was stacked too high.

Four

Jenny arrived early to the club and warmed up at the driving range. The grass was immaculate, and each player's practice rectangle was stocked with professional, expensive balls gleaming white under the morning sun. The course's range balls were more costly than the ones she'd brought to play all eighteen holes.

She'd never played the Quail Hollow Club, but the lush, trim grounds spoke to the golf course's prestige—and cost. Even if she knew a member who could make a proper recommendation for her to join, she couldn't fathom or afford dropping a hundred grand initiation fee followed by monthly dues.

She warmed up with air swings and hip rotations, then used her seven iron. Each ball sailed a smooth flight. Wow. She'd missed the feel of hitting the sweet spot and watching the white speck lift high into the air.

The daily grind of work often interfered with her beloved hobby, but the sport also reminded her of her father, and so she'd avoided those bittersweet memories. Her youngest recollections were of scavenging for abandoned tees around the tee boxes or fixing her father's divots on the greens. When she could hit the ball consistently straight at the age of eight, she'd joined him on the course. By twelve, she'd become a bogey player off the junior tees and earned the privilege of driving the golf cart. By high school, he watched her play competitively. By college, he still traveled to her games to support her.

When her father's cancer had relapsed and spread, he'd declined further treatment and entered hospice. She'd spent his last few months near him. When he was finally at peace, she let her career plans dictate her life's schedule, and the sport that had dominated the first twenty years of her life became a memory to reflect back on.

On the range, she switched to her driver and let herself enjoy reminiscing on pleasant childhood memories of time well spent with her father.

"I don't believe I've seen a finer swing."

She turned to see Beau standing behind her, looking casual in black slacks and a light blue Polo shirt. Despite his good looks, she planned to enjoy defeating him in golf even more so than she did in the courtroom.

"Thank you. Are you a member here?" she asked.

"I'm flattered you'd think so, but I don't have enough old money to afford this place."

"It's gorgeous."

"That it is," he said without taking his eyes off her.

Warmth rose in her body. She slid her driver back into her bag.

"Ready for a little friendly competition?" he asked, something of a tease in his drawl.

"Ready."

Before she could protest, he scooped up her golf bag and carried it to the cart. She preferred to walk when she played golf, but weekend etiquette usually meant a cart to keep the pace of game going and prevent delays. With that in mind, she noticed that Quail Hollow was nowhere near as crowded as she'd expected for a Saturday. She wondered if that was due to the exclusivity of the club.

Beau loaded her bag on the golf cart beside his. In front of their cart, two men dressed in khaki shorts and collared shirts watched her.

"Jenny Wiley, this is Jeremy Riddler and Buck Lander. They are our competition today."

Jenny cordially shook their hands as she reflexively glanced at their golf bags. TaylorMade irons and drivers. Well-used. Probably not casual players. How much money was involved in today's game? Judging by Riddler's Rolex, he didn't play for pennies.

"Pleasure to meet you," Buck said, squinting at her with a wrinkled face framed by short gray hair. "Beau says you're about a five handicap."

She opened her mouth, but Beau placed a hand on her shoulder. "I might argue for more because she hasn't played in a while."

"Buck Lander," Jenny said. "Any relationship to the Landers who own half the car dealerships in Charlotte?" She suspected this man was the Quail Hollow member in this foursome.

"Owner and CEO." Buck beamed.

"We're up," Jeremy said, all business. As he hopped into the golf cart, morning sun reflected off a bald spot on the top of his head.

Jenny turned an expectant glare on Beau. "Five handicap? I'm a scratch player on a bad day," she said in a harsh whisper.

Beau grinned. "I know that. My assignment of your handicap isn't meant to be an insult. Buck's a sandbagger. I'm just leveling the playing field."

After she slid into the cart beside Beau, he drove them up the path and parked beside the first tee box.

She roughly pulled a glove onto her left hand and cinched the Velcro strap. "We're playing on the same team."

"I'm glad you picked up on that."

"You said if I win, I don't have to involve myself in your case." She already knew she'd help Karl's case, and it scared the hell out of her—what with a ghost being involved. But Beau had no way of knowing she would acquiesce when he'd made the deal with her yesterday.

"That deal still stands," he said.

"But if I lose, you lose. So, either way, you lose—either in golf or getting my help on the case." She adjusted her visor.

He grinned. "Darlin', I'm playing golf on an exclusive course on a sunny May day with a beautiful woman. I've already won."

Did this over-the-top charm really work on women? Of course it did. Her knees went weak anytime she felt his eyes on her, much less when he was dishing out compliments.

She knew nothing of Beau's personal life, but if the way women drooled around him in the courtroom was any indication, he had his pick. As Charlotte's most eligible bachelor—handsome, rich, and charismatic—he could probably have a different woman every month.

"Besides," Beau added, "we're going to win. And I have eighteen holes to convince you to take the case anyway."

She would make him work for it, she decided. She wouldn't let Beau know she'd already started reading articles about Cecilia's murder. But Jenny would have to go back to Karl and pull his sister's ghost away from him so she could ask the woman who killed her and why, an undertaking Jenny dreaded.

An elected official, Cecilia had said.

The very idea that someone in power might be responsible made Jenny's blood chill. Getting involved was going to be bad news, but she couldn't allow an innocent man to be charged with murdering his sister.

And how was she going to reveal the real perpetrator to Beau when her source was the murder victim?

"What's the wager?" she asked, determined to clear her mind of Cecilia and Karl long enough to enjoy the golf outing.

"Ten thousand to the charity of our choice."

"Ten thousand dollars?" Jenny's mouth fell open.

To charity? That part was unexpected. No matter who won today, the winner got bragging rights and a charity benefitted. She hadn't pegged Beau as having an ounce of philanthropy. Charity didn't fit with the self-important personality she'd assigned to him from their courtroom interactions ... unless donations helped him clear his conscience.

BEAU SHOT third off the first tee box and was pleased to watch his ball sail down the middle of the fairway ahead of the others.

"You've got a nice swing," Jenny said.

"From a player of your caliber, I take that as quite a compliment. Tell me, you could've gone professional. Why not?"

They climbed into the cart, and he drove her to the women's tee box.

"I wanted to be a lawyer. In fact, I always wanted to be a lawyer," she explained. "My father was a judge and my inspiration. He'd tell me courtroom stories—no names of course—and I knew I wanted to be a prosecutor."

She pulled out her driver, lined up her ball, and swung. Her motions were smooth as silk, and the ball soared two-hundred fifty yards down the fairway.

She looked positively scrumptious in khaki shorts and a pastel pink shirt. The clothing hugged her form while exposing smooth legs tapering to narrow ankles. Her hair was in a low ponytail, more relaxed compared to her usual courtroom bun. Strands were starting to curl slightly under the humid Carolina sun.

He'd researched her months ago when she'd beaten one of his partners on another case. She'd attended Greenville University in law school, but more interesting was her participation in competitive golf in college. Since then, he'd wondered if he could create an opportunity to watch her play.

By the fire in her eyes, she was enjoying his company. She might not like him as competition in the courtroom, but outside of it, her body language suggested she wasn't dissatisfied spending time with him.

Their co-golfers cast skeptical glances at Jenny's drive. Beau and Jenny hopped back in the cart, and he drove toward their balls. Jenny twirled a tee between fingers of her left hand. He'd seen her do that in the courtroom, except with a gold-colored coin.

"It's a shame you spend so little time at a game you're obviously very good at," he said. "But the world is lucky to have a lawyer like you."

"Why on earth did you involve me in your case?" she asked.

Changing the subject. *Hmm*. She became uncomfortable whenever he complimented her. Because she didn't like admiration or liked it too much?

He enjoyed being open with her and intended to keep their interaction honest, whether it made her squirm or not.

"You're hiding something." The slight dilation of her pupils told him he was right. "You have some type of intuition. I can't figure it out. For a while I thought perhaps it was a unique viewpoint on cases. I thought you poured over information from police reports to coroners' reports to forensics and could somehow see things others missed. But then I took you into a case cold yesterday, with minimal background information, and you could still see the truth."

Her throat bobbed in a swallow, and he hated the look of fear this discussion put in her eyes.

He pressed on, "I don't understand it. I'd like to, but judging by how your body stiffens the more I discuss it, I'm guessing it's your little secret. So, if you don't want to share, I'll respect that. But I'd be most appreciative if you use that gift to help my cousin Karl."

She shot him a look. "Cousin?"

"Cousin." He slowed the cart to a stop near the golf balls and hopped out, walking around to his bag.

Beau plucked out his iron and took his fairway shot. The ball landed pin-high, just to the right of the green. He could make par on this hole.

"One-hundred-seventy yards to the pin with the wind," he told her.

BY THE NINTH HOLE, Jenny and Beau held a two hole lead over Jeremy and Buck. They stopped at the clubhouse for refreshments and sandwiches.

Jenny sipped an ice-cold rum and Coke. She'd been relaxed and enjoying conversation with Beau between shots —sports, politics, and courtroom antics. She'd shoved thoughts of Cecilia's dead eyes away. Today was about golf, normalcy, and pretending her life hadn't changed forever.

"They want to press on the back nine," Beau said.

She gave a nervous chuckle. "Um. I can't cover a ten-grand bet, much less twenty."

"I'll cover it, but we won't lose."

Taking another sip of her beverage, she mulled the

unpleasant thought of the large sum Beau would owe if they lost.

Seeming to notice her discomfort, he changed the subject and shared tales of his wild childhood, complete with juvenile detention as he drove them toward the tenth tee box.

"I learned how to avoid legal trouble, but life was still a game, even through college," Beau said.

"A game, huh? Fraternities, college parties, women?" Jenny teased.

"All of the above."

"Seems you haven't changed at all."

His eyes widened in mock shock. "I am deeply offended you hold me in such low esteem."

"Hmm. So, that wasn't you on the home page of the *Charlotte Observer* dressed in a tux on your way to a gala with a twenty-year-old knock-out model on your arm?"

He smiled, apparently flattered she'd seen and remembered the photo rather than offended that she was accusing him of still being a frat boy. "Julia is a friend's daughter. She's actually eighteen, and I've never in my life dated a woman more than five years younger than me."

"I was merely observing that she's young and pretty," Jenny said, covering her surprise. Had she misjudged him?

"She is both of those things. Very young and spirited. Which is why my friend asked me to be a chaperone. A lot of things can go wrong in a night of fun—either damaging to her reputation, her father's reputation, or her own safety." He took a bite of his sandwich.

"Chaperone and bodyguard?" Jenny sipped her drink, thinking of how the man's priorities were not what she'd imagined. Seeing decency where she expected ego, disoriented her.

He pulled the cart behind Jeremy's and lowered his voice while the other men prepared to take their shots. "Many confrontations can be solved with mediation and cooperation. Others can't. I have a good sense of people—when to patronize, when to negotiate, and when to threaten. You have to know when to push back so you don't get pushed around."

"You're talking about manipulating people."

"I'm talking about *managing* people. It's only manipulation if all the benefit is one-sided."

Jenny considered his words. "You're saying you know the difference between when to keep the peace and when to throw down?"

Leaning closer, he said, "I started life as a young hothead, and my behavior led to criminal activity. I ran with a rough crowd for a bit. So, yes, I know when to use kid gloves, when to use boxing gloves, and when to use brass knuckles." Standing, he walked around and pulled his driver out of his bag.

His words carried an earnestness that made her believe him. She sensed anguish and regret were woven into his checkered past. Interest and intrigue had her wanting to know more, but she didn't want to probe painful memories.

She stood and leaned on the cart. "Do you deny you still like to party and live life carelessly?"

He set up his ball and drove it down the fairway. "I'm in bed every night by ten and up for court the next day." He spoke as innocently as a choir boy before lowering his voice.

"I'm neither careless with my life nor casual with my relationships."

Jenny swallowed.

He slid his club back into his bag. "I believe you've drawn some harsh and erroneous conclusions about me, counselor."

"I guess I have." And her judgments had helped form a comfortable armor against his charm, but now that was slowly dissolving. "Did you always want to be a lawyer?"

He drove them toward the women's tee box. "No. My partying days ended when my older sister died. It was time for me to grow up and earn a decent living. I thought long and hard about what I wanted to do with my life. Ultimately, what appealed most was defending kids like me so they'd have a chance to straighten their lives out like I did. I became prelaw, and the rest is history."

"I'm sorry about your sister."

He stopped the cart and regarded her, head cocked to one side. "It was sixteen years ago. No apology necessary."

Down the fairway, Jenny and Beau watched their competition take their next shot. Jenny cringed for the hundredth time at Buck's loopy swing. Buck cursed when he hit an unintentional slice.

"It's an interesting backswing," Beau whispered. "Somehow, the ball still usually manages to go straight."

When Beau and Jenny reached their balls on the fairway, Beau parked and pulled out his five iron. "Got any tips for me?"

"Don't wear white shoes after Labor Day?" Giving him a saccharine smile, she took another sip of her rum and Coke before setting it back in the cupholder.

"Funny."

"You need to rotate more," she added. "You tend to slide your hips through a bit. Better rotation will add more distance on your ball—another ten or twenty yards."

Beau stood over his ball after lining up his shot. "Isn't this the part where you place your hands on my hips to demonstrate proper motion?"

They'd been on such friendly terms all day that she could easily imagine letting her guard down and standing close behind him—guiding his hips through an imaginary shot. She had to remind herself Beau was the enemy. A wolf in Jack Nicklaus's clothing.

"This isn't *Tin Cup*, and I'm not Kevin Costner," she replied, pulling a club out of her bag.

"Pity." He took the shot, rotating perfectly. The ball landed at the back of the green. "Well, look at that, coach. You should give lessons."

"I have no desire to be around a bunch of sweaty men wanting 'hands-on' lessons." She lined up her shot.

"What do you desire?" Beau asked.

She froze over her ball and tried to focus. When was the last time a man asked her what she wanted?

She swung. "*Crap*. Pulled it." She knew the instant she'd contacted the ball.

"It might be okay." Beau squinted against the sun.

"It's wet."

The ball splashed into the water hazard.

"Yup. Wet. My bad. I distracted you," he said.

She stabbed her club back into her bag and slumped in the cart. Beau drove them down the fairway toward the green. She was more irritated by her reaction to his simple question than by the question—what did she desire? She struggled with the question all too often. Dating only ever seemed to expand her long list of things she didn't want rather than clarify what she did.

"I don't know what I desire. I have a list of anti-desires from men I date. No lying, cheating, or stealing. No using creative artistic talent as an excuse against gainful employment. No talking down to people in customer service—if a date can't be polite to wait staff, there'll only be one date. No dead-beat dads." Since she was thirty-two and dating men around her age, some would be divorced with children. She wasn't opposed to dating fathers, but they needed to be mature about their family. "If he's divorced, it better be resolved. If he can't reconcile with the ex or seeks only to have minimal visitation with his child, that's a pass."

Looking at the empty rum and Coke in the cup holder, she groaned. "I honestly just said all of that out loud." She wanted to dive off the golf cart and bury her head in a sand trap. "Alcohol just dissolves my filter. I'm mortified."

Beau chuckled. "I was asking what you desired in life, not just from a relationship. But should I ever ask you out on a date, I'm now fully briefed on your expectations."

She groaned again as he stopped on the cart path near the green.

"You're okay to keep playing?" he asked.

After pulling out her pitching wedge, she sashayed to the drop point. "Mr. Montrose, I'm going to drop my ball, take my penalty stroke, sink this chip, and still make par."

He grinned at her sass. "Yes, ma'am."

Smiling despite herself, she was amused at how a very Southern *"yes, ma'am"* could carry such subtle sexual undertones.

She wished the only thing she had to think about today was golf and a handsome flirt—not murder, not ghosts, and not Karl sitting in a holding cell.

Five

Beau loaded Jenny's clubs into the trunk of her Prius. His Tesla was parked a few rows away. He thought about remarking on their environmentally conscious choice of vehicle, but he suspected she'd tease him about driving a luxury car.

"Thank you for coming," he said.

"I had a lot of fun," she admitted. "And we won!"

The alcohol had worn off after four holes, and she hadn't had divulged any more personal information. Pity.

"Do I still get that Greek dinner?" she asked.

Dang. He definitely wanted to take her out, and he recognized the effort she was making. "I can't tonight. I have a family obligation."

He inwardly winced at her look of disappointment followed by her awkward silence of vulnerability. Taking her hands in a gesture of reassurance, he said, "Tomorrow night. I promise. I'll even be nice to the wait staff."

She drew her hands away as she bit her lip. "Tomorrow. Tomorrow I need to see Karl again."

"You're going to help me?" He'd taken a gamble keeping talk of the murder off their golf conversation and it seemed to have worked.

She met his eyes. "I'm going to help Karl."

Beau bristled at her tone and that she felt the need to make such a distinction—she was helping Karl, not him. He hated the moments when she suddenly remembered to fall into her usual habit of treating Beau like the enemy. Four hours of leisure had melted some barriers, but years of opposition weren't erased in a day.

"I'll make arrangements for us to see him," he said.

"I need to speak with him alone."

He resisted the urge to feel slighted. The key was that she was willing to help. He'd let her do that on her own terms.

Reaching up, he adjusted the pendant around her neck where the clasp had worked its way around to the front. He hadn't expected the gesture to feel intimate and certainly didn't make a habit of touching women's jewelry. But his hands seemed to gravitate toward her of their own volition, drawn by something he couldn't quite control.

"Okay. Alone," he consented. "Then I'll take you for Greek as promised. We'll throw in some baklava for good measure."

That earned him a quirk of her lips—sweet, tender, and almost sinful in their allure.

He dropped his hands and stepped back, chastising himself. What was he thinking, wanting to kiss the assistant DA? And if he had, would she accuse him of seducing her into helping him with Karl's case? That was certainly not

Beau's intention. Would she add it to her list of "nevers" with men?

Never date a man who kisses you after you agree to help an accused murderer.

"Dinner tomorrow." She nodded, distracted, and got in her car.

Slipping his hands into his pockets, he watched her drive away.

Greek dinner. Baklava. Maybe over the meal he could talk her into another round of golf or possibly a real date, preferably one that wouldn't involve overconsumption of onions.

BEAU ARRIVED HOME, dropping his keys and wallet on the counter. Golf today had been particularly enjoyable. He was already wondering when he could convince Jenny to join him again, maybe they could make it a regular weekend outing.

He glanced toward his office to the right of the foyer. Mounds of work waited for him.

"Hey, Dad, you're back. Want to shoot some hoops?"

Work could wait. If Travis wanted to spend time with him on a Saturday afternoon, Beau would choose quality parenting over lawyering.

"Yeah, I'll meet you outside."

Beau left his golf clothes on and slipped into a pair of running shoes. Outside, he joined Travis at the basketball hoop anchored in the brick wall above the garage doors.

They started with two-point warm-up shots.

"What'd you shoot today?" Travis asked.

"Seventy-seven." Beau smiled at his score, five over par, but had been more impressed with Jenny's two under. "We beat the competition."

Beau had tried to convince Travis to take an interest in golf, but the teenager preferred basketball. As long as the kid was engaging in some type of sports, he was fulfilling the household rule of exercise and activity.

"Who'd you play with today? Criminals or cops?" Travis liked to harangue him about representing criminals.

Beau recognized the banter as a way for Travis to connect with his father figure. Beau took no offense, as he didn't socialize with convicted felons. He would never have drinks or play golf with someone like Bubba Hollins. Some of Beau's friends had misdemeanors, but he didn't judge people based on a few instances of poor judgment as such an action would be hypocritical of him.

"I played with an assistant district attorney."

"Oh? Another lawyer? Was he any good?"

"She." Beau wriggled his eyebrows. "And yes, very good. Scratch golfer."

"Cool." Travis rimmed and sunk a three pointer. "Is she cute?"

"Yeah, she's cute. I like her."

Beau trotted in for a layup and tossed the ball back to Travis.

"Are you going to date her?" Travis asked.

"Maybe."

"Prom is coming up." Travis dribbled the ball.

"Oh? You got a date?"

Beau's chest tightened slightly. He had a unique relationship with his nephew. When his sister died, leaving Travis behind, Beau had been a wild college kid, though still an improvement over his more troubled youth. When he'd held Travis for the first time—a small bundled baby—and learned he was the boy's custodian, he'd straightened up his act almost immediately, determined to give the boy the happiest childhood he could provide. At least, the happiest childhood possible without a mother.

He'd made every aspect of Travis's life playful, rarely strict. He seldom raised his voice and never played the tough-love father figure. He just gave love.

His spare-the-rod-and-spoil-the-child technique probably clashed with some other parenting styles, but Travis responded well to learning by example instead of fear. Rather than being spoiled and taking advantage of the leniencies given to him by his uncle-turned-father, he took the lessons of love from Beau and applied it to his own life.

Now, he was a teenager talking about prom.

He'd also begun to take more of an interest in Beau's personal life. Beau wasn't sure if that had to do with him not being Travis's biological father. Travis couldn't be jealous if Beau dated a woman, because it in no way represented disloyalty to Travis's mother. However, Beau suspected Travis's curiosity had more to do with the boy becoming a man and taking an interest in women himself. Travis could ask questions about women, feigning interest in Beau's love life while actually applying and adapting the answers to his own.

Travis took a shot, but it lipped out.

"Wait." Beau grabbed the ball and held it. "I remember you telling me Kelly Lander accepted your prom ask. Don't look so nervous. The hard part's over if she already said yes." He made the shot, earning a satisfied nod from Travis.

Travis retrieved the ball. "I don't know about that. Now I have to show her a good time."

"It's prom," Beau said. "If memory serves, having a good time is dancing."

"Yeah." Travis shot again, missing off the rim. "I don't know how to dance."

Beau grabbed the basketball and turned to his son. "Right. I guess we never got around to dance lessons. Well, there's no time like the present." He held the basketball out in front of him, parallel to the ground.

Travis glanced around nervously. "What are you doing?"

"Take hold of the basketball. We'll both hold it, and I'll take you through a waltz."

Travis hesitated before tentatively placing hands on either side of the basketball close to Beau's.

Beau counted off the steps and guided Travis through the waltz with a four count. When neighbors walking their dogs passed by with quizzical looks, Beau waved congenially and chuckled at Travis's reddened cheeks.

JENNY WAS CURLED on the sofa watching television when her sister called.

"Jenny's answering service," she said dismally.

"Let me guess. Wine and *Alias* reruns?" Phoenix asked.

Jenny groaned into the phone. "Worse."

"Uh, oh. Ice cream and *Alias* reruns?"

Jenny took a bite of her mint chocolate chip ice cream and didn't answer her sister.

"That bad?" Phoenix pressed. "Work or relationship?"

Jenny paused the show. Where to begin? "I spent half the day with Beaufort Montrose ... playing golf."

"Beau? Isn't he the defense lawyer you can't stand? I thought you hated him."

"I never hated him. He was the defense lawyer I couldn't stand. Now, he's the defense lawyer I need to stop ogling."

"What changed?"

"Spending time with him outside the courtroom. He's actually a nice guy when he isn't defending criminals. It's appalling." Jenny swallowed another bite of ice cream, savoring the small bits of dark chocolate.

"So, you're attracted to an attractive guy. Big deal. You need to enjoy the time you have in this life. *'Every person's happiness is their own responsibility.'*"

"Really? You're going to throw one of Dad's Abe quotes at me?"

"And if Beau has you playing golf again, that's another win."

They seldom spoke about how Jenny had lost interest in the sport after their father died. She'd grown up playing golf with her father, and she hadn't made the time to play out of fear it would churn painful memories. But playing today had been different. She'd enjoyed golfing with Beau, and the few times she'd thought of her father was in fondness for the time they'd shared on the course.

"Is Beau attracted to you?" Phoenix asked.

"I don't know. I had a rum and Coke and shared a little too much. I told him all the reasons I dump guys."

"What'd he do?"

"Laughed at me." Jenny jabbed her spoon into the mound of ice cream.

"How so? Laugh like *you're-a-bit-crazy* laugh, or laugh like *you're-so-cute* laugh?"

"Both, I think. Anyway, it doesn't matter. I'm about to get involved in this ghost's murder. I can't even fathom a relationship if I'm seeing ghosts."

She didn't know if Beau would reject her, have her committed, or laugh at her, and she didn't want to find out what his reaction would be.

"Dad found Mom. It can happen."

"I don't know how you build that kind of trust with someone."

"Golf is a start," Phoenix offered, though a little too tentatively to be convincing.

"Maybe."

How do you date a man whose cousin's freedom depends on you talking to the dead?

Jenny walked to the jailhouse feeling as though she was swimming upstream through a cascade of emotions—as if trying to hit her driver two hundred yards into the wind without landing short in a water hazard.

She'd enjoyed yesterday's outing with Beau. He'd been an engaging conversationalist and nothing like the self-aggrandizing persona she'd witnessed in his courtroom performances and media coverage.

Then she'd humiliated herself with a list of traits she disliked in men, followed by reminding him he owed her dinner, which somehow sounded like a date. And that wasn't factoring in the latest ghost complication.

At the jail, Jenny checked in to see Karl and was led deeper into the building to the consult room. She tried to brainstorm a way to signal Cecilia to come with her without looking insane, talking to a ghost.

When she approached Karl in his bright orange jumpsuit, alarms rang in her ears. No Cecilia. If she wasn't with her brother, where was she?

Jenny sat across from Karl as he scanned the room, presumably looking for Beau.

"I'm alone. But Beau knows I'm here."

"Okay. Are you going to help him?" Karl's voice carried a pleading edge.

Oof. The tone tugged at her emotions. "Yes."

"You believe me? You believe I'm innocent?"

"My belief is irrelevant. What matters is what we can prove."

"Your belief matters to me. It obviously matters to Beau, and Beau sees through people. You have to earn his respect, and he respects you."

Karl's words struck her like an arrow. For some reason, Beau's impression felt significant. She could ponder why later.

"Yes," she said. "I believe you're innocent."

Karl's shoulders relaxed slightly.

"Did Cecilia have some sort of client log? Or maybe

somewhere she'd keep confidential or sensitive information?"

He snorted. "Like a little black book? Honestly, I don't know. I was hoping the police would uncover something on her laptop—anything that would point to motive somewhere other than me."

Jenny could review police records on Karl's case, but because Beau had recruited her help, she'd assume for now that not much evidence for others' motives had been discovered.

"What were some of her favorite places to visit?" Jenny asked, ostensibly to look for a "little black book," but also to find Cecilia herself.

Jenny imagined if she lingered as a ghost, she would spend the time visiting her favorite spots.

He listed a few parks and restaurants and then added, "Her favorite place was that park off McDowell Street."

"Marshall Park?" Jenny asked for clarification.

"Yeah. She liked to feed the ducks on the pond."

If she didn't find the ghost at her apartment, Jenny would try Cecilia's favorite areas. If that failed, plan B would require seeking help, because she had no idea how to intentionally summon a ghost.

Karl fidgeted with his handcuffs. "If my freedom depends on finding dirt my sister may or may not have kept on clients, I don't think I have much of a chance."

"It's a little more substantial than that, but I can't make any promises."

Jenny knocked on Cecilia's apartment door, quietly calling the ghost's name. She couldn't go inside the crime scene, but perhaps she could coax Cecilia out if she was lingering inside.

"She ain't home." A neighbor stepped partially into the hallway from his apartment.

"Oh, okay." Jenny backed away from the door.

"She ain't coming home. She was murdered. It was in the papers." He eyed Jenny suspiciously as though she was some sort of debt collector.

"Ah. I'll be on my way."

Jenny left the apartment building and drove to Marshall Park. There, she spotted the woman immediately, as her attire wasn't commonplace for a park. Cecilia hovered near a bench, thankfully out of earshot of the people enjoying the warm day. Jenny didn't want to be overheard having a one-sided conversation, especially one about murder.

As she approached the woman, sunlight streamed partially through Cecilia's apparition. The scene might have been beautiful if it wasn't so disconcerting.

Here goes nothing.

"Hello, Cecilia."

The ghost jumped, stumbled backward, and unleashed a piercing scream that surely would have made the nearby ducks spontaneously explode if they'd heard it.

Jenny clamped hands over her ears and took a non-confrontational seat on the bench. Did Cecilia think Jenny was here to hurt her? She was already dead. And weren't humans supposed to be the ones screaming at the sight of ghosts, not the other way around?

"Can I introduce myself?" Jenny asked when the scream tapered into a prolonged squeal like a bad set of brakes.

"Oh my gosh. Oh my gosh. Oh my gosh! You can see me!" Cecilia flapped her hands in excitement so vigorously Jenny half expected her to lift off the ground.

Rubbing at her ears, Jenny squinted up at the hysterical ghost. "And hear you."

"Wait. I know you. You visited my brother in jail. You're Beau's girl!"

"Um, there are so many things incorrect about that last sentence."

"*Woman*. Whatever." Cecilia waved a dismissive hand.

"I'm not Beau's woman."

"Oh, you just wish you were." Cecilia smirked.

Jenny scowled. "I'm here to help your brother."

Cecilia raised her hands in surrender. "Okay, okay. Sorry to offend. Just saying. There's not a woman in Charlotte who hasn't had a few smoldering thoughts about that man. Am I wrong? Too bad he doesn't indulge a little more often."

"With you?"

Cecilia stared at Jenny as though she was the bizarre ghost lurking among the living. "No. Are you ill? He's my cousin."

"Right. Fine. Let's refocus. Your brother."

"Poor Karl. Nobody should have to perform CPR on their kin. I tried to tell him I was already dead, but he couldn't hear me. How can you hear me?"

Jenny pinched the bridge of her nose. Keeping Cecilia on track was going to be a challenge. "Just lucky, I guess," she grumbled. "I don't know why. My father could see ghosts. Now I can."

"That's so cool. It's in your DNA or something."

"Or something. Anyway, because I can see you, I thought I'd try to help Karl."

Cecilia placed her hands on her hips. "You're not doing this to impress Beau?"

Jenny leaned forward. "Let me be clear. I could lose my job helping a defense attorney on a homicide case my office will be prosecuting. I could be committed to an insane asylum for talking to a ghost. I'm doing this to keep an innocent from being convicted of murder. Not sleeping with Beau. Not to advance my career."

The ghost raised her hands again. "Easy. Easy. I pushed the wrong buttons there. I apologize. I saw how you reacted when Beau touched your shoulder. Clearly, I misread the situation. Please help my brother."

Jenny straightened. "Let's start with who killed you."

Six

After closing herself in her apartment, Jenny sank onto her couch and buried her face in her hands. Her heart was still hammering from Cecilia's earth-shattering revelation.

She couldn't do this. She was an ADA, not a detective. How could she possibly follow through with her promise to help Karl? How could she not? As the only one who could see the victim's ghost, she was the only person in position to help him.

Her world spun like a relentless merry-go-round. Up. Down. Round and round. She'd never had a panic attack—well, except the night before the LSAT, and maybe sometimes before golf tournaments—but definitely never one lasting this long.

Reaching into her pocket, she grasped her father's coin. Courage, wisdom, justice, temperance. She drew a slow, steady breath, and her angst began to ebb.

The chime of her phone dragged her out of her thoughts.

Beau, *Pick you up or meet you there?*

Right. Greek dinner with Beau.

Not feeling well. Will have to take a raincheck, she typed with shaking thumbs and pressed SEND.

Beau, *I can bring it to you. Or drop it off.*

She sighed. Why couldn't he be the self-important jerk she'd pegged him for all this time? Instead, he was incredibly likable. Still, she couldn't face him now, not after learning the killer's identity through ... paranormal channels.

'And how did you come to learn this critical piece of information, counselor?'

'A freaking ghost, that's how.'

Impossible.

Thirty seconds after she pressed SEND, Beau called her phone. She sent the call to voicemail with shaking hands.

Yeesh, he was persistent. Somewhere in the distraction of messaging him, her heart rate finally normalized. She needed a long, calming shower, time to gather her thoughts, collect herself, and form a rational plan.

BEAU KNOCKED on Jenny's apartment door and waited impatiently for her to answer.

When she opened it, she was dressed in blue jeans and a Charlotte Hornets t-shirt. Her blonde hair hung damp around her shoulders.

"What are you doing here?" She glanced around him as if checking to see if he was alone.

Who else would he be with?

"You didn't answer my calls."

"I was in the shower." She tried to sound irritated, but he noted an edge of defensive worry.

"You didn't call or text back." Too worried about her to wait for an invitation, he stepped into her apartment. Because he'd come directly over instead of picking up dinner, he was empty handed.

"Stop pushing me," she snapped, but she closed the door rather than ordering him to leave.

"I'm pulling. You're the one pushing." Backing off was not a trait he'd ever possessed.

A trace of fear crept into her expression, though she made no reply.

He raked a hand through his hair and paced the living room, cluttered with haphazard stacks of novels and throw blankets. It was as messy as her office.

Was she afraid of him? He would get to the bottom of this.

"I called Karl this afternoon. He said you stopped by and seemed nervous, asking about Cecilia. Karl is a nervous guy, so I thought maybe he was projecting. Then you cancel our dinner on me. Then you shut out my calls."

"I'm allowed to want a night alone. We barely know each other. You can't barge into my place demanding answers."

He stepped closer. "Look me in the eye and tell me something about this case hasn't upset you."

She backed away and wrapped her arms around herself as she met his gaze. Her brown eyes were wide, almost pleading Beau to drop the subject. He could have laughed at the absurdity of the unasked question, except her distress drained the moment of any humor.

"The case upset me," she admitted, her voice carrying a defeated tone he'd never heard before.

"Why?"

She sat on her red sofa, a sharp contrast to the beige carpet beneath it. "Beau, you seem like a nice guy."

"I'm glad we established that." He sat beside her, close enough to prevent retreat but careful not to touch her.

Her lips quirked. "I don't even know how to tell you this."

"Just say it. Rip away. Like pulling a Band Aid. I haven't asked you out on a date, so it's not like you're breaking up with me. What about the case upset you?"

"I assure you, your heart is safe."

"Jenny, what's going on?" Confident in his instincts, he took her hand. Soft, warm. And he had the satisfaction of seeing her shoulders relax slightly.

"DA Stu Winslow killed Cecilia Dixon."

JENNY STARED down at their joined hands. With Beau beside her, her anxiety eased. The situation remained daunting, but his touch inexplicably gave her strength.

Maybe she shouldn't have told him, but she didn't want to be alone with this bomb shell. Looking into his eyes, she saw calculation but not disbelief.

"Who is your source?" he asked.

"I can't tell you."

"Okay. You're protecting someone. I get that."

She was protecting herself. She couldn't start spewing about the existence of ghosts.

Giving her hand a brief pat, he stood, clearly feeling slighted at her keeping the source to herself.

"What evidence do we have?" he asked.

"Currently, nothing."

Beau paced her living room once again. She enjoyed his presence in her personal space. Under different circumstances, she might have enjoy it more. The sparks she'd felt playing golf together had been replaced by the bitter truth —she was seeing ghosts now, and no sane man would maintain a romantic interest in her.

"We need evidence." He rubbed the back of his neck.

"Yeah," she agreed. "I was thinking you could review the police reports with an angle toward the DA while I look into another lead."

"Another lead?" He paused mid stride.

"Cecilia had client information. Damaging information. I need to retrieve her data source."

After the park, Jenny should have gone directly to retrieve it, but learning the killer's identity had shaken her and she'd retreated to the safety of her place, alone.

"Karl told you this?" Beau asked.

"No." Jenny would skirt around the ghost source, but she wouldn't lie. When this was all over, no matter what happened, she'd be able to say she'd never lied to Beau.

He frowned. "Right. Your source. If you have someone who knows this kind of damning information, they need to come forward."

"That is not going to happen," Jenny said emphatically.

"We can give him or her protection."

"I work for the system, and I'm a little afraid for my own safety." More than a little.

He stopped and stared at her. "Then we need to stick together. Go over the evidence together and retrieve the information Cecilia had together."

He wanted that information. Jenny could see it. His fingers twitched as her unease escalated. Did he want the records to vindicate Karl, or because of what they might reveal? Did the city's top defense attorney have secrets of his own to protect?

"Separate," she said.

He tilted his head to one side and studied her. "Jenny, you can trust me."

Could she? Did she know that for certain? She wanted to trust him, but honestly, she barely knew him.

His lips pressed together as his expression darkened. "Fine. Separate. Can you get the information by noon? We'll meet up at lunch."

She shook her head. "I have meetings and motion hearings. We can meet after work."

"Greek?"

Her favorite food wasn't nearly as appealing with a murder case to discuss, but she did want to keep their next interaction public.

She agreed to the restaurant meeting.

BEAU LEFT Jenny's apartment feeling unsettled. A mysterious new source had emerged and claimed the real perpetrator was Stu Winslow. Truth or ulterior motives?

He walked down the stairs and toward his car. Outside, a sheet of night sky twinkled with stars. The earlier humidity of the day had abated.

He believed Jenny's claim to have an informant and didn't think she was capable of attacking the DA's credibility without cause. But what if she was being manipulated by this unknown person? Beau had difficulty believing anyone could manipulate Jenny.

When he reached his car, he sat inside as his fingers drummed against the steering wheel.

Now this mysterious source suggested a hidden cache of damaging information belonging to Cecilia, and doubts were cast. Based on Jenny's reaction, she suspected he might have something to hide.

He didn't, and her unspoken suspicion stung. He'd had to control his frustration and remind himself that he hadn't earned her trust. Not yet. He wanted to be with her when she found this list, not because he feared whatever information it contained but because Jenny could be in danger if such a list existed and if she wasn't the only one searching for it.

When he pulled onto the road, he called one of his contacts. Matt handled delicate jobs for him, always quiet, competent, and discreet.

jobs for him, always quiet, competent, and discreet.

"Matt, I need you for a job."

Stu Winslow cruised his yacht away from the shoreline of Lake Norman. The late Sunday sun hovered over the horizon. As long as he kept the boat at around ten knots, the breeze tempered the sweltering heat. North Carolina seemed to have skipped spring entirely and sped right into summer.

He savored the rare weekend alone, when he could indulge in the finer things in life. Working sixty hours a week took its toll. Which was why he needed the lake house and the boat. A refuge.

All of it had been threatened the night the hooker had tried to blackmail him. His secrets were safe now. She'd carried them with her to the grave.

The irony of the situation was that none of this was Stu's fault. He was a hardworking, red-blooded American. He'd simply overextended himself. He had a certain image to maintain, and inherent expenses accompanied that image. He'd done well as a tobacco attorney, but then, the cost of two divorces nearly broke him.

Naturally, Stu had engaged in certain illegal activities to keep from going bankrupt. But no one was hurt by these endeavors. Honestly, some crimes shouldn't even be considered crimes.

Who was Cecilia to enforce punishment for those indiscretions? She'd had no right. He'd done the only logical thing he could do under the circumstances. And he was likely one of many victims she'd been blackmailing. In the end, he'd done society a favor.

When Stu's mobile phone rang, he cut the engine and reached for the device. He hesitated when he saw blood stains smeared across his palms and fingers. He rubbed his hands together, trying to rid them of the crimson. When he blinked his eyes, the blood had vanished.

He answered the phone. "Hello?"

"Hey, I just wanted to give you a heads up about some strange activity."

Stu recognized the voice of one of the jailers. As district attorney, he had eyes and ears everywhere, a necessary advantage in his position. "I appreciate that. What has you concerned?"

"The accused in your murder case had a visit from his lawyer."

"No big surprise."

Even the legendary Beau Montrose couldn't win this case. Every piece of evidence pointed to Karl Dixon as the murderer. And Stu intended to make sure it stayed that way. He rarely tried his own cases because he had a team for that, but this particular one required oversight in the interest of self-preservation.

"Yeah, but Mr. Montrose brought Jenny Wiley with him."

"My Jenny Wiley? My assistant DA?" Stu asked.

"Yeah. That's why I thought it was strange. I figured I could wait until the week to tell you, but then she came back alone today without Beau."

Red spots danced in Stu's vision as his rib cage tightened around his lungs. His mind worked furiously, searching for a calm and rational explanation for why Jenny would be inserting herself into his case without first discussing it with him.

"Okay. Thanks for letting me know." Stu ended the call and slammed the phone down on the boat's console.

Jenny already had her moment of glory with the Bubba

Hollins case. What was she playing at by visiting Karl Dixon? Was she after Stu's job?

If he'd overlooked some loose ends concerning Cecilia's death, was Jenny going to ruin him by uncovering new information? The DA's office didn't call her the Wiley Coyote for nothing. She had a prideful intuition about cases, much like her father had.

Stu would confront the ADA about it tomorrow. If he didn't like the answers she gave, he would be forced to consider other measures for extracting information from Jenny Wiley. And if she started poking her nose where it didn't belong, well ... accidents could happen.

Seven

Jenny didn't sleep well, but coffee the next morning gave her the drive and motivation she needed to push through her morning schedule. She arrived at work a half hour early, finished paperwork and emails, followed by a motion hearing.

She looked up when a knock sounded at her door. Darby, one of the city's homicide detectives, entered. She wore navy slacks and a fitted T-shirt, sporting her badge and gun visible on her hip.

"Hi, Darby. Come on in."

She entered with a bright smile against her dark skin. "I heard you're the big mama on campus. You had a huge win in the Bubba Hollins case. And against Beaufort Montrose no less."

"Thank you. I do enjoy beating that particular defense attorney," Jenny said.

How had she moved past the Bubba case so quickly? It was such a career success from only a few days ago. But since then, Jenny had a new challenge in life—seeing ghosts. Fortunately, Cecilia hadn't made an appearance yet today.

"You only like defeating him in the courtroom though, right? Local gossip has you two spending a little time together."

"Beau asked me to look in on a case."

"The Karl Dixon case? The slam dunk?" Darby raised a brow. "I hope you're not planning to stir things up there."

Jenny folded her arms over the only bare spot on her desk in front of her keyboard. "I am only ever after the truth."

"Good. Then you won't mind me talking to you about the Schertz case."

Jenny leaned back with a frown. She knew the case and understood exactly why Darby was here. The DA's office refused to prosecute. "You can talk." She gestured to the vacant chair across from her desk. "I can listen."

Darby didn't sit. "DA Winslow won't prosecute. We need to put this criminal behind bars."

Schertz had allegedly murdered his business partner around the same time five million in diamonds went missing. Mr. Schertz claimed his partner stole them and that whoever he stole them had likely killed him.

"You don't have a solid case," Jenny said, not intimidated by the cop's tactics. She'd reviewed the file last week and was forced to back Stu's decision on this one. The DA's office didn't prosecute on could-have, should-have, or would-haves.

"He has means, and he has motive," Darby shot back.

"Be that as it may, you have no strong evidence. No DNA on the murder weapon. And you don't even have the missing diamonds. Come back when your work is finished," she added politely.

Cecilia flickered into the room, causing Jenny to flinch.

Darby gave her a questioning look.

Jenny waved a dismissive hand. "Hiccups. Sometimes they come on violently."

Cecilia smacked her gum. "I couldn't help but eavesdrop. I mean, your day has been mind-numbingly boring until someone brought up murder—you know—other than mine. The diamonds are in Mr. Schertz's fish tank."

Jenny pursed her lips, leaned forward, placing her elbows on her desk, and rubbed her temples. "Is there anywhere you haven't looked?" she asked Darby.

The detective crossed her arms. "We know how to do our job."

Jenny ignored the barbed tone. "Didn't Schertz have an exotic fish collection? Tong-something?"

"Blue Tang."

"There you have it. A fish tank might be just the spot to hide five million dollars' worth of uncut diamonds."

"Oh, I see how you did that," Cecilia said with a sly grin.

Darby scowled but turned to leave.

"Bring us the evidence, and we'll bring the justice," Jenny called after her.

After the detective left her office, Jenny checked her watch. She was due for another meeting in ten minutes. She gathered her things. "I have a conference. Can you make yourself scarce until we go fetch your book?" she asked the ghost.

"Why? You don't want any more violent hiccups?" Cecilia cackled, shaking her head and vanishing.

On her way to the conference room, Jenny passed DA Winslow in the hallway. He didn't look like a killer—mid-fifties, squeaky-clean, professional, and bright-eyed. He was arrogant, but few achieved his status through mediocrity and humility.

Jenny looked down at her phone, pretending to text and walk while hoping to go unnoticed by Stu.

"Jenny."

When Stu paused to talk, she stepped out of flow of traffic and slipped her phone into her suit jacket pocket beside her coin.

"Stu." Her heart knocked against her ribcage. Was she standing two feet from a murderer? What if Cecilia remembered incorrectly? Was a ghost's memory infallible?

"I heard you visited a defendant," Stu said. "Someone I'm trying to put away for murder."

Did the DA have spies in the jail?

She shrugged, determined not to reveal the flight response she kept at bay as he towered over her, crowding her space. They conversed in a public place; nothing untoward would happen here, she reassured herself.

"Beau asked me to speak with Karl Dixon."

"Beau?" Stu's eyes narrowed.

"Beau Montrose."

"Yes, I know who Beau is. I didn't realize the two of you were on a first name basis."

"We're amicable outside of the courtroom." Images of his warm, brown eyes and infectious smile steadied her.

"What did he want from you regarding the defendant?" Stu asked.

"Just to talk with him." Jenny tried to sound casual, though cold sweat trickled down the back of her neck.

She slowly slipped her hand into her pocket and touched the medallion. She silently asked the question that would probably doom her career: *Did Stu Winslow murder Cecilia Dixon?*

Guilty, came the reply.

Her knees weakened, and she leaned slightly against the wall to keep herself upright.

"Hmm. I'm sure you wouldn't interfere in my case." The DA's green eyes turned dark and toxic looking.

"Of course not." Bringing the real killer to justice wasn't interference—it was doing her job.

She thought of one of her father's favorite Abe Lincoln quotes:

"I am not bound to win, but I am bound to be true. I am not bound to succeed, but I am bound to live up to what light I have. I must stand with anybody that stands right, and stand with him while he is right, and part with him when he goes wrong."

A prosecuting attorney had an obligation to the truth.

Resolved not to let Stu Winslow intimidate her, Jenny straightened. "Curious though that you're personally taking this case. Anyone from the Homicide Team could handle it."

His eye twitched as he glanced down at his palms before

rubbing them against his suit. "Don't interfere," he reiterated before turning and striding away.

DURING HER LUNCH BREAK, Jenny drove toward the cemetery where Cecilia said the notebook was hidden. The ghost plunked herself down in the passenger seat.

The awkward silence grated between them, and Jenny felt compelled to fill it. "We'll get the notebook, and expanding the suspect list will cast reasonable doubt on Karl as the perpetrator," she reassured Cecilia.

"We only have each other." Cecilia fidgeted with the bangles on her wrist. "Our parents died in a car crash. Karl became the responsible older brother and," she hesitated, "I became his problem."

"Why become an escort?" Jenny asked. "It seems like you could've had a number of different career choices."

"Youth and stupidity. I started with alcohol after my parents died and escalated to heavier stuff. Somewhere in there I fantasized about being a gorgeous call girl with high-society clients pampering me. I was going be Julia Roberts, and Richard Gere would show up and change my life forever." She let out a humorless chuckle. "Life isn't a movie. Some of the guys were nice, and some were manipulative jerks. My options were to get tough and use their dirty deeds against them or be swallowed alive."

"Or build a new life," Jenny suggested delicately.

"Or that. But I didn't see it that way through my drug-induced haze."

"It doesn't seem like Karl would ever let you fall that far. He loves you very much."

"People can only help you if you let them. I wouldn't let Karl help me. He was always the older brother who knew better than I did. It was maddening—him playing parent all the time. You and your sister seem to have a good relationship."

"Oh? How do you know that?"

"I see bits and pieces. You and Phoenix keeping in touch even though she lives in New York. You flew up there when she was heartbroken over some guy. You don't tell each other what to do."

"We did plenty of that for the first twenty years of our lives together." Jenny smiled to think of her father's Abe Lincoln quote whenever she and her sister had argued. "*A house divided against itself cannot stand,*" he would say. That had been their cue that they'd pushed his temper to the brink and it was time to quietly sulk to their rooms or feign civility. "But we learned how to be friends, and now we're best friends."

"What changed?"

"When our father's health declined, all of our petty arguments disappeared."

"That's good. You should hang onto that. You and Phoenix have something special."

Jenny felt a pang of sympathy toward Cecilia and the weight of responsibility. Her success or failure on this case would determine Karl's future and Cecilia's justice.

. . .

JENNY PARKED at the cemetery where Cecilia's parents were buried. They walked past rows and rows of tombstones on their way to the crypt.

"My first amateur sleuth assignment, and I'm in a cemetery. With a ghost. This is unbelievable. Why hide your notebook in a cemetery?"

Cecilia's hips swayed as she walked beside Jenny. The attorney wasn't sure which was more unsettling—a ghost *walking* beside her or *floating* beside her. Perhaps it didn't matter. Cecilia's outfit was more distracting than her swagger.

"It's the perfect hiding spot." Cecilia said. "I can come here anytime I want, and everyone assumes I'm here to mourn my parents. Which isn't entirely untrue. But I figured no one would think to look here for my notes."

"You stored your secrets creepily in a cemetery, and you hid your notebook so well that no one would find it unless you happened to come across someone who could see you as a ghost."

"Well, obviously I didn't think I'd die before I got to use all of the power in my book."

"Why a notebook anyway?" Jenny asked. "Why not a jump drive? You can encrypt the information and have access to your secrets anywhere."

Cecilia snorted. "So says the attorney who keeps a typewriter so she can create documents that can't be stolen electronically."

Jenny frowned. "How do you know that?"

Cecilia had seen her office but couldn't know *why* Jenny had a typewriter.

The ghost shrugged. "I dunno. Stuff pops into my head

now and then. I can't control what I see about other people. And it's pretty random."

They reached the crypt. The rectangular stone building had a tile floor and an arched ceiling.

"If you remove the small marble piece here, there's a little hollow space behind it where I keep my notes."

Jenny worked her fingers around the rectangular piece of tile, then glanced at Cecilia's long acrylic nails. With a sigh, she reached into her pocket and pulled out her key fob with her apartment key attached.

"Any day now, counselor." Cecilia sighed impatiently.

"You have a slight advantage to pulling out objects like this with those long, strong nails of yours. There's barely any space between this tile and the surrounding wall."

Cecilia looked at her nails, flicking the tips against one another. "Do you always complain this much?"

"Only when I'm coerced into helping a wrongly accused man and trying to retrieve vital evidence under the duress of having no idea how to have this information 'miraculously' discovered in a logical way."

In lieu of a reply, Cecilia placed her hands on her hips and smacked her gum.

BEAU SPENT the morning at the district court, pacing the hallway, soothing clients, and chatting with prosecutors. This was followed by negotiating a plea in a case of driving under the influence and telling a relieved client about the outcome.

By eleven a.m., he was back in his office reviewing his

team's files on various cases. The room was his pristine sanctuary, complete with plush gray carpet and a light blue couch. An imported Brazilian cherry desk was centered between matching bookshelves. His desk held two monitors, a phone, a keyboard, and not a speck of dust. One wall was decorated with signed Master's flags from golf legends—Tiger Woods, Jack Nicklaus, and Arnold Palmer.

Beau responded to an email from a panicked client before switching gears when someone new called in, begging for a criminal defense attorney. At last, he had a few quiet minutes to draft pleadings and prepare for a different upcoming case.

As his fingers raced across the keyboard, his phone buzzed with a text message.

Matt, *Got time for an update?*

Beau called him. He rose from his desk and walked to the window, pacing as he looked out over the city. The dominating buildings were The Vue, tall and bulky, and the tapering Bank of America Corporate Center. The May sky was an endless bright blue, void of clouds.

"Matt, what news?"

"Is she mourning someone?"

"Not that I know of. She lost her father, but that was years ago. Why?" Beau asked.

"She spent the morning at her office, but now she's at a crypt. Not her father's."

"Curious."

"Yeah. And she walked through the place talking to herself. I was too far back to hear what she was saying."

"Any chance she was using earbuds?"

"No. And what's more curious is that she has another tail."

"Someone else is following her?" Beau's pulse quickened. Was Jenny in some type of trouble? Perhaps her strange behavior had nothing to do with Karl's case and was related to some other issue in her life.

"What do you want me to do?"

"Stay on Jenny. This new tail sounds like trouble. Text me the cemetery address, and I'll head that way. I do not want the assistant DA identifying you or learning I sent you to follow her. Maybe I can get a look at whoever is following her and confront her about it."

He snatched his keys off his desk and strode out of his office.

AT LAST, the tile loosened. Jenny reached inside a space just large enough for her hand and withdrew the notebook —a denim-blue pleather book, well-worn, with loose pieces of colored paper and bits of napkins sticking from all sides. A thin rubber band wound around it, barely keeping all of the contents contained.

"This thing is in worse shape than my office."

"Sorry, counselor," Cecilia sassed. "I didn't have time to index the contents before I was stabbed to death."

Jenny flicked the edge of a pink napkin dangling out of the book. "Napkins?"

"Hey, you gotta write crap down or you'll forget it. I bet you don't walk into a courtroom without a legal pad or something."

Jenny had no response to that.

She envisioned Cecilia scribbling down notes on a napkin with red lipstick before stuffing it into her bra. Maybe Jenny should be handling this thing with gloves to protect herself.

She inspected the width of the book. "How many people do you have dirt on?"

Cecilia grinned. "Sooo many people. Sooo many juicy secrets."

Jenny recited one of Lincoln's quote, "*Nearly all men can stand adversity, but if you want to test a man's character, give him power.*" She rubbed at an ache forming in her chest. "I think I'm going to be sick."

"Not in my parents' crypt you're not."

Jenny glared irritably at Cecilia. "You realize every person in this book has motive. This might incriminate Stu, but he'll be lumped as a suspect along with everyone else."

"Then it should be enough to cast doubt for Karl's jury —if it goes to trial."

"Yeah, you're right." Jenny felt the weight of the book in her hand. "Now, I need to get this discovered. Ideally, it should be discovered here, I think, for authenticity. However, I can't put it back yet. I need to copy it first in case something happens to the original." Copying it discretely, would be another challenge.

"And if you have to reveal your copies?" Cecilia asked. "How are you going to explain that?"

Jenny blew her blonde bangs out of her face. "No idea."

When she stepped out of the crypt, midday sun assaulted her eyes, making her squint.

Movement flickered to her right.

She began to turn when Cecilia yelled, "Look out!"

Shrinking back, Jenny simultaneously tried to duck and pivot at the same time when something struck her head. Pain exploded through her skull and reverberated through the bones of her face and jaw.

Her vision blurred as she collapsed to the ground. Momentarily blinded by pain, she couldn't see her attacker.

"Hey, you!" an unfamiliar man's voice shouted from a distance.

Footsteps shuffled close to her and then retreated.

"He's taking the book!" Cecilia cried. "Go after him! He's taking the book!"

Jenny tried to push herself upright, but a wave of nausea pinned her in place. She rolled onto her back, blinded by a bright sky as her vision swam before everything went dark.

Eight

Beau knelt beside Jenny as she lay on the ground, eyes closed. He kept fingers on her pulse at the wrist—strong and steady.

"She took a pretty good blow to the head," Matt said.

"It's not bleeding, at least not externally," Beau noted as he gently palpated her scalp. "And this guy bludgeoned her and then took off?" he asked his hired covert private investigator.

"He was about to hit her again when I hollered at him and scared him off, but not before he took something. Left her purse, but grabbed something else she dropped when he hit her. I couldn't see what it was while I ran to her."

Matt wore khaki pants and a pale violet short-sleeve button-up shirt. He was short with an average build and clean-shaven, round face. Nothing remarkable showed in his facial features. He was the perfect guy for covert work. Nondescript, nonthreatening.

"So, this wasn't a robbery, at least not for money." Beau

gently ran fingers over the bump on Jenny's head as he debated whether or not to call for an ambulance.

What was she doing in a cemetery? And what did she have in her possession that someone would assault her to steal?

"And you didn't get a good look at the perpetrator?"

Matt shook his head. "Hoodie and sunglasses. Medium-height, medium-build, white guy. That's all I got."

Jenny stirred.

"Why don't you take off?" Beau said quietly. "I'll handle it from here. Let's keep you anonymous."

Matt nodded. "I appreciate that. Do you want me to keep tailing her?"

"That won't be necessary. She's not leaving my sight until I know what the hell is going on."

When Matt left, Beau brushed his fingers lightly through Jenny's bangs. "Jenny?"

She slowly blinked her eyes open, struggling to focus. "Beau?"

He enjoyed the way his name sounded, like a sigh of relief. "Jenny, can you sit up? Are you hurting?"

She allowed him to help her into a sitting position. Her face was pale, and she was sweating on the hot concrete.

Confusion washed over her expression, and she sucked in a sharp breath. "The book? Where is the book?" Her eyes and hands began searching her body and the ground around her.

"Easy. Take it slow and easy, Jenny. Whoever hit you took your book."

Jenny glanced at him warily, as if briefly considering if

he could've been the perpetrator. Then, she tilted her head to one side and then relaxed.

"Let's get you to an ER and have a doctor examine you."

"No, I have to get the book back." She stood unsteadily, and Beau guided her to a nearby bench among the graves.

"I don't know what this book is about, but it's not worth risking your life for. You took a serious hit. It knocked you unconscious."

Jenny shook her head as they sat together. "No. The blow didn't knock me unconscious. I passed out from pain."

"Either way, you need medical attention."

"There's no time. He'll destroy Cecilia's book if I don't stop him."

"Cecilia's book?" Beau thought about where Jenny was laying after the attack. She'd been outside the crypt where Karl and Cecilia's parents had been laid to rest.

Guilt knotted his stomach. He'd involved Jenny in his case, and now she was injured because of it. And what was she doing investigating?

"You came here to retrieve a notebook that belonged to Cecilia?" He asked carefully. "Is there something in there that can exonerate Karl?"

Jenny touched her hand to the back of her head and winced. "Yes, she kept incriminating notes on her clients. Blackmail material. We have to get it back."

"Get it back from whom?"

Had she actually seen the attacker? Matt certainly hadn't been able to identify him.

"Stu. Stu Winslow took it."

Beau frowned. "Are you telling me that Charlotte's district attorney assaulted you in broad daylight in a cemetery to steal evidence that could make him a murder suspect in an ongoing investigation?"

"Yes. No?" She tilted her head slightly.

Was she not sure? She'd better be damn sure if she was going to level an accusation like that.

"He didn't take it himself. He sent someone to take it from me."

Stu Winslow hired somebody to tail her? That made more sense. Matt had explained that the man following Jenny had crept to the outside of the crypt and then hesitated, uncertain. He'd texted and waited. When Jenny had emerged, he'd pounced.

"Right now, we have no way of proving any of this ties back to Winslow," Beau said.

Jenny swallowed. "Not without that book."

"But if it lists all of Cecilia's clients, it won't specifically identify Stu as the killer."

"Let's get out of the cemetery." Jenny took a shaky breath and stood.

They walked together past the gravestones.

"You're right," Jenny said. "That's why you need to look for any clues or unexplored leads in the police reports that might suggest Stu's involvement. But your client doesn't need us to specifically identify the actual killer. Karl needs us to create reasonable doubt. He could have committed the murder, but so could several other people with stronger motive."

Beau stayed close as they walked, ready in case she collapsed again. While her reasoning was sound from a legal perspective, Beau wouldn't limit his objective to solely exonerating his client if it meant leaving someone out there who tried to harm Jenny over what she knew. And just how much did she know?

"What incriminating evidence against Stu is in the book?"

"I don't know. I didn't have a chance to read it. I planned to make copies and figure out how to get the evidence discovered."

"Discovered without exposing your confidential informant?"

"Something like that."

He ground his teeth. She was far too tight-lipped about this informant—who apparently told her about the crypt but failed to show up and left her vulnerable. Why hadn't he or she come with Jenny to retrieve the book? A darker thought crept in. Maybe this person had set her up.

"You need that informant to come forward," Beau said. "If he or she knew where the book was kept, he or she may know what was inside the book."

Jenny let out a soft, bitter laugh. "Oh, she knows what's in that book. But she *cannot* come forward."

They reached the lot where their vehicles were parked side by side. She eyed his Tesla beside her Prius, but didn't make a comment about the cars.

She began to fish in her purse for keys.

Beau leaned against his car. "You're not driving."

"This is my car. I need to go get that notebook."

As soon as the keys were in hand, Beau swiftly took them.

"Hey!" she protested.

"Maybe I can't force you to get medical attention after getting clocked on your noggin', but I'm not letting you get behind the wheel."

She stepped forward to reclaim her keys, but her knees buckled. Beau caught her, clamping down his frustration at her stubbornness. Although she up-righted quickly and defiantly, he kept one hand on her elbow for support.

She jerked it back and smoothed her skirt. "Fine. Perhaps I shouldn't drive." She rubbed her temple. "I need water and ibuprofen."

He opened the passenger side door of his car for her. "I happen to have both of those at my place."

She sighed, muttered, "Cecilia" with exasperation, and slid into the seat.

Beau did a double take at Jenny speaking the name of his cousin—the name of the victim. He hadn't been close to Cecilia, but he did have some childhood memories and had attended her funeral. He'd probe Jenny's word later when she wasn't suffering from a head injury.

JENNY RUBBED the swelling on the back of her head. She'd never been attacked before today. She decidedly preferred watching violence on the show *Alias* to having it invade into her real life.

She was scared, but pissed-off more than anything. When she'd learned Stu was the culprit, she'd been afraid of losing her job, not being assaulted. Now she felt more determined than ever to nail the DA—murderer, criminal, violent offender.

If Beau hadn't arrived, would her attacker have finished her off? A chill rippled through her body despite the afternoon heat.

"How did you find me at the cemetery?" she asked.

Beau's grip tightened on the wheel. "Who is your informant?" he countered.

From the back seat, Cecilia smacked chewing gum in the back seat. "Beau paid someone to follow you."

Jenny gaped at him. "You put a tail on me?"

"How did you—?"

"Did you take the book?" she demanded. "Was this all a ruse? Helping Karl when what you really wanted was the book?"

Cecilia rolled her eyes. "Girl, you have trust issues."

Jenny snapped her mouth closed and crossed her arms, still feeling a sting of betrayal from Beau's actions.

"No," Beau said firmly, shaking his head. "It's nothing like that. I had you followed because I was worried about you. You did a complete one-eighty over the last few days. One fine day we're talking and connecting over golf, the next day you're pushing me away over the case. Something has you scared."

"Damn right I'm scared. That still doesn't give you the right to have me followed."

"Get over it," Cecilia cut in.

"If you opened up to me, I wouldn't have to resort to putting a tail on you." Beau's voice rose with frustration.

"I don't trust anybody right now," Jenny said quietly.

"Maybe it was a beat too far and not my finest moment," Beau relented. "I had you followed over concern about you, no my own interests."

Cecilia made a disgusted noise. "A handsome, single man saves your life, and your response is to give him grief?"

Because Beau couldn't see or hear her, Jenny resisted the urge to snap back at Cecilia.

She clutched her purse in her lap as several beats of silence passed between them. "Thank you for rescuing me," she said to Beau in a calm, even voice.

He reached his right hand over and held hers. "You're welcome. Let's get you feeling better, then I'll help you get the book back."

His hand felt solid and warm. She needed solidarity and warmth right now to ground her. She wanted his help and his strength. But when Cecilia divined the current location of the notebook, how could Jenny explain how she knew exactly where it was without also divulging the existence of Cecilia's ghost?

"I'm sorry I accused you of taking part in my attack. I'm not myself right now." Unless this was her new self—testy from seeing ghosts and living in danger because of the secrets she learned from them.

"Apology accepted," Beau said. "I'll allow a few unsubstantiated accusations after a scare like that."

He pulled into the driveway of a four-bedroom red brick house with white columns and parked in a three-car garage. His other cars were a green, beat-up pick-up truck and a blue Honda Accord.

Jenny looked at the cars and then back at Beau. "Those are not the cars I expected to see in your garage."

"Oh?"

"An Aston Martin. Maybe a Porsche."

Beau chuckled. "Sorry to disappoint you, but every

Southerner needs a vehicle for hauling—hence the pick-up. And the Honda belongs to Travis."

"Travis?"

"His son," Cecilia blurted.

Jenny glanced at Cecilia as she followed Beau into his house. "Oh, a son."

"Technically, his sister's son, but Beau raised him," the ghost added.

"Oh, nephew." Jenny recalled Beau mentioning his sister's death as a turning point in his life. Now she understood why.

Beau eyed her skeptically as he led her into the kitchen. The large space had tall, eggshell colored cabinets and a wide stove with a mosaic tile backsplash of blue and white. A marble-topped island sat in the center of the room.

Beau fixed ice wrapped in a thin towel for her.

"He's old enough to drive?" Jenny asked.

"Sixteen," Cecilia answered.

"Sixteen," Jenny repeated. "And you raised him on your own?" She took the ice from Beau and pressed it against the back of her head as she sat at the counter bar stool.

Her impression of Beau had changed so dramatically over the last three days that it made her dizzy. When she focused her gaze back on Beau, he was leaning on the counter, watching her.

"Somehow," he began slowly, "I feel like you just had an entire conversation that didn't involve me, even though I'm the only other person here."

Jenny gave a nervous chuckle and glanced at Cecilia. "Must be the head injury." She kept the ice firmly in place.

"I might fall for that explanation if your strange

behavior hadn't preceded your trauma." He arched an eyebrow as he assessed her, obviously waiting for a better explanation.

She couldn't give him a better explanation—not without sounding certifiable.

"Why didn't you mention you had a son when we played golf?" she asked.

"We didn't get that far in the conversation. I'm sure it would have surfaced over dinner."

The elusive dinner, Jenny thought. The date she would never be able to have because of her ability to see ghosts.

She set the ice down on the counter. "I need to get that book."

Beau dumped the melting ice in the sink and then poured her a glass of water from the refrigerator. "Okay. We'll go fetch it. Together."

"Beau," Jenny groaned.

"Head injury. That requires twenty-four hour monitoring, right?"

"Is that really a thing? I'm not sure that's a thing."

"And," Beau continued, "you're obviously in danger. I'm not letting you walk into that alone. Whoever you're up against is willing to use violence."

She thought about his comment the other day about knowing when to use brass knuckles. She wanted help, but even with a ghost helping, success wasn't guaranteed. Bring Beau into the fold would make him the third wheel, and Jenny would keep slipping up, like she had when learning about Travis while talking to Cecilia.

Beau stepped around the counter, turned her chair

toward him, and placed gentle hands on her shoulders. "Let me help you."

The compassion in his eyes softened something deep inside her. She stood and stepped into his arms. His embrace felt so soothing she thought she could stay there forever. Maybe just a few minutes longer.

"Tell me about your son."

As Beau spoke, Jenny felt the deep, soft reverberation in his chest. "He's a good kid. Best thing in my life. He's responsible and ambitious. He aspires to be a doctor one day, so he's taking advanced math and chemistry."

"You have life all figured out, don't you?" she said softly. "The job, the family, the hobbies."

He brushed his thumb along her cheek. "I don't have it all figured out, but I do have a lot of hard earned gifts. Would be nice to share what I've built with someone."

Jenny leaned back, just enough to look up at him. The heat in his gaze made her melt further in his arms. His hands slid up behind her back to cradle her head and draw her closer. Kissing him seemed so simple. In this moment, kissing Beau offered a solution to everything—or at least an escape. Their lips were tantalizingly close.

"Um. Am I interrupting?"

Jenny startled and turned to see a wide-eyed teenager standing in the entryway between the kitchen and the living room.

Clearing her throat, she stepped back from Beau as heat spread into her cheeks. He didn't appear embarrassed in the least.

"Not at all," Beau said easily. "We were just heading back out. Travis, this is my friend Jenny Wiley."

Jenny smiled politely. "Hi."

"Hey. Oh. Uh, Dad, I was going to go to the gym to shoot hoops with Monty and a few guys. Can I take the car?" The boy hooked his thumb in his jeans pocket.

"Yes. No problem. Jenny and I are working on a case."

Travis grinned, gaze bouncing back and forth between the two of them. "Working, huh?"

"Working," Beau said. "You finish your homework?"

"Almost done."

"Okay. Leftovers for dinner tonight."

Beau turned back to Jenny. "Ready to go?"

"Restroom?"

"Down the hall and on the left. I'll meet you in the car."

JENNY LOCKED herself in the bathroom to freshen up and gasped when she saw her reflection. Her blouse was wrinkled and half untucked while her bun was, well, not so much a hairstyle as a bird's nest.

She had no right seeking solace in that man's arms when her life was so messed up. And his reaction when Travis walked in? Beau was comfortable being seen close to her while she was keeping secrets from him.

After she made herself presentable, she softly called, "Cecilia?"

The ghost shimmered into view within the mirror, superimposed over Jenny's reflection. She stifled the urge to scream.

"Check it out. I can appear in mirrors," Cecilia said.

"Fabulous," Jenny deadpanned. "Listen. Beau isn't going to let me do this alone."

"I know. He has this whole macho protector vibe. I love it."

"The point is that you and I need to communicate more discretely. I can't look like a lunatic talking to thin air if I'm going to work with him."

"It probably was a bit awkward, us chatting about Travis."

"We need a signal. Instead of me making eye contact, I'll strum my fingers to indicate you and I are communicating."

"Okay. Cool. I got it. What's the signal for me to tune out when you're about to kiss the hunk again?"

Jenny sighed. "I don't even know how to respond to that."

"Hmm, I'll just use my best judgment." Cecilia winked at her.

"Please don't."

Cecilia's voice softened. "You know you two make a cute couple, right?"

Jenny exhaled quietly against a tightened throat. "Sure. Until he finds out I talk to ghosts. Then he'll want nothing to do with me."

Nine

Stu clasped the notebook in his hand as he leaned back in his desk chair at his home office. He'd had his deliveryman bring it here because he couldn't be seen in the man's company anywhere near his office.

Edges of the notebook were worn, as was the spine. It appeared as though it had been moved in and out of a coarse location resting on its back instead of an upright position on a bookshelf. Of course, it had to be placed in that position. If it had been placed upright, all the little haphazard pieces of paper and napkins would've fallen out.

Stu skimmed the material—a staccato collection of names and notes. Some he recognized and others he didn't. Some decipherable and others not. There were politicians, cops, lawyers, judges, and business owners mixed in with the criminal element, and all guilty of some crime according to Cecilia's note.

How had she collected so much information? She must have had many sources—drug dealers, other clients, and other prostitutes. Somewhere in here, he suspected she had dirt on him.

Glancing at his watch, he stifled a frustrated groan. He didn't have time to sort through this information right now. And he hadn't yet spotted any particular notes she'd recorded pertaining to himself, but they were buried somewhere in it.

He considered his options. If he burned the notebook, any incriminating evidence against himself would be forever destroyed. However, if he kept it, how much was the information worth to the other parties involved? How much of his own debt could be paid if Stu blackmailed others with Cecilia's secrets?

He stored the book in a secret compartment in his desk with plans to return and examine it more carefully after tonight's dinner.

He stood and massaged his hands together as he walked to his room to shower and dress for his dinner date. The blood stains kept appearing and disappearing throughout the day, but he was becoming more accustomed and less bothered by their presence. Surely once Karl was convicted and this nightmare behind Stu, his imagination would subside, and the blood would permanently disappear.

BEAU SAT in his car in his garage and waited for Jenny.

He'd never been so flummoxed by a woman in his life. She'd transitioned from reluctant to participate in Karl's case to trying to solve it entirely on her own. Based on her cagey behavior, her actions had nothing to do with impressing him. In fact, she seemed determined to keep him at a distance in every moment today, except for just now in the kitchen.

And, wow, he'd wanted to kiss her. His rational brain tried to veto the outlandish impulse. He didn't need this type of bizarreness in his life. She was messy and indecisive. Although, she was also a phenomenal golfer with a smile that made him feel like a million dollars—when he could actually coax one out of her.

When she joined him in the car, she looked more composed. They sat for a moment in silence.

Gripping steering wheel, he asked, "Where to?"

"Right." She strummed her fingers on her thigh. "Where to?" Her voice trailed.

Was she asking him?

Before he could clarify, she rattled off an address.

"That is very specific," he said, entering the address on the touch screen of his car.

"It's Stu Winslow's house."

"You know the DA's home address?"

"I do now," she said on a heavy sigh.

Her anguished tone quieted his urge to press her harder on the topic. Backing out of his driveway, he headed toward the district attorney's neighborhood.

Beau slipped on a pair of sunglasses, partly to keep the late afternoon sun from blinding him and partly to conceal his irritation. He tried to remain patient, but Jenny obviously had no intention of opening up to him.

When he stopped at a red light, the silence stretching between them blanketed the air with tension.

"How do you plan to take the book back?" The light

turned green, and Beau moved his foot to press the accelerator.

"Wait!" Jenny threw out her left hand and grasped his thigh.

He immediately shifted his foot back to the brake. In the intersection, a diesel truck barreled through a red light. If Beau had accelerated at the light change, the truck would have rammed his car.

His heart leaped into his throat at the idea of barely avoiding disaster. His fingers trembled on the wheel. A half-second difference and Travis would've been an orphan.

When the intersection cleared, he drove cautiously through. At the next parking lot, he turned in, parked the car, and let the air conditioning run. More than a little unnerved by events, he was ready to demand some answers.

He snatched off his sunglasses and turned toward her. "What the hell was that?"

She shrank back but didn't appear surprised by his outburst. She fidgeted with the hem of her skirt.

"I'm not taking you anywhere until you give me some answers." He watched her carefully, hoping she wouldn't decide to just get out of his car and leave. He couldn't stop her if she did.

"Okay. I'll give you answers." Her voice sounded defeated, but her gaze was resolute. "I'll answer all of your questions, and we'll find out if you can handle the truth."

She turned toward him in her seat. "The reason I have *intuition* about people's guilt or innocence is because I have this." From her blazer pocket, she pulled the coin Beau had seen her hold in the courtroom on occasion. "I think of a question in my mind and the coin gives me an answer: innocent or guilty."

He took the coin and inspected it. On one side was written the four virtues: JUSTICE, COURAGE, WISDOM, and TEMPERANCE. The other side displayed the picture representation of each: scales for justice, an owl for wisdom, a lion for courage, and a man sprinkling water into a jug of wine for temperance, or moderation.

"My dad gave it to me," she added.

"Judge Wiley." Beau ran his thumb over the surface of the medallion. Based on the worn edges and dull color, the coin was old. "He had a reputation for fairness but toughness."

Jenny nodded. "He always knew the guilty from the innocent. He claimed the coin belonged to Abe Lincoln. I don't have any proof of that, but it doesn't change what it's capable of."

He handed the coin back to her. "Show me."

Her eyes widened. "What?"

"Ask the coin if I stole a 1975 red Camaro on my fifteenth birthday."

She swallowed as her grip closed around the coin. "Not guilty."

"That's right. It was white."

"Guilty."

An eerie sort of chill prickled his skin. "You're the only one who can hear the voice in the coin?"

"That I know of. I haven't exactly passed it around at parties."

"And you used the coin to determine Karl's innocence?"

"Yes."

"And avoiding the collision just now? How did that happen?" he pressed.

She sighed. "That was different. Cecilia warned me." She rolled the coin between her fingers. "She's my confidential informant. She was beside Karl in the conference room the first time you took me there—well, her ghost, obviously, because she's dead."

"Cecilia's ghost told you where the book was hidden in the mausoleum?" Beau struggled to grasp what Jenny was saying, because it couldn't be right. Ghosts didn't exist ... yet what else might explain the things Jenny knew?

"And she warned you about the truck running the red light just now?" he asked.

"Yes." Jenny looked hesitant, like she expected Beau to through her out of his car at any moment.

"And she's here now?"

Jenny glanced toward the backseat. "Yes, in the back seat with her arms crossed, chewing gum, and telling me how this is taking too long."

Beau hadn't seen Cecilia in years, but he recalled her fondness for gum and that patience wasn't one of her virtues. Still, he couldn't understand Jenny's tactic, talking about ghosts as if they existed.

"How did she know to warn us?" he asked.

"I'm no expert in all things ghostly—Cecilia is my first time *seeing* a ghost—but they can sometimes catch glimpses of the future."

"The idea of ghosts is ... outlandish." Beau rubbed a hand over his face. He had dozens of more questions, but he didn't want to continue grilling Jenny like a witness on the stand.

Her demeanor was that of resignation; she clearly didn't expect him to believe her.

"Is this a ploy to get rid of me?" he demanded, the words coming out harsher than he'd intended.

"You asked for the truth," she shot back. "It's not my fault if you can't accept it."

"Do you hear yourself? You're telling me there's a ghost in the back seat of my car."

"You're cousins. What is something only Cecilia would know?" Jenny countered.

He scratched his chin. "Family reunion. I was eighteen, so Cecilia would have been twelve. Who got drunk and streaked naked through the park?"

"Uncle Theo. Apparently that wasn't a first for him."

Beau sat stunned and speechless as the seconds ticked by. Jenny hadn't even hesitated to answer his question.

"Forget it. I need to get the book." She reached for the passenger door handle, clearly intending to leave and work alone again.

"Jenny, wait. Maybe I don't fully comprehend what you're saying, but I'm still not letting you do this alone, or with only a ghost." He put the car in drive and pulled back onto the road.

She leaned back, closed her eyes, and exhaled. "Thank you."

JENNY TOOK off her seatbelt when Beau parked across the street from Stu Winslow's house. During the drive, she'd let her anger at the cemetery attack simmer until it burned hot and focused. She was ready to confront Stu.

"Slow down," Beau said. "We need a plan. We don't even know if he's home."

The house was three stories of gray stucco with black framed windows. The late afternoon sun cast light on a yard of healthy, manicured lawn and large crepe myrtles blooming vibrant pink.

"He's home," Cecilia said and proceeded to divulge the exact location of the book.

"Cecilia says he's home," Jenny told Beau. "The notebook is in a desk drawer in his home office."

"Okay," Beau said carefully. "Let's think through the play here? We can't be caught breaking and entering. Let me send my guy in there."

"Your guy?"

"I have a friend who does discreet work for me. His ethical code is a bit more flexible than most."

"The same one who tailed you earlier," Cecilia added. "I'm going to go spy on Stu."

To Jenny's relief, Cecilia vanished.

Jenny tugged on one of her earlobes as she addressed Beau. "You're saying your PI would have no objection to breaking into Stu Winslow's house and stealing the book?"

"That's right. And if we do it my way, neither one of us is culpable. Yes, we conspired to commit a crime, but my guy would never divulge his payment source. And he knows if he ever got caught doing a job for me, I'd represent him without charging legal fees."

"This is a new level of shadiness for me." Jenny shook her head, feeling a weight of hopelessness sinking into her bones.

"It's better than you or me breaking in there," Beau replied. "And you certainly can't knock on the door and confront a murderer. My friend will handle it. He's helped me on several cases, sometimes even vindicating my clients because we uncovered the real perpetrator."

"What sort of tasks have you employed him for?" Jenny asked.

Beau pursed his lips. "You can wipe that judgmental look off your face and the skepticism out of your tone. He gathers information for me. That's all. Sometimes he has to enter places he's not supposed to enter in order to get the information I need for clients. Sometimes he has to follow people to get that information. He does not fabricate any false information. He does not plant evidence. I would never ask him to do that, and even if I did, he would refuse. Like you, I'm committed to discovering the truth. I just use more creative methods on occasion."

Nodding, she felt the weight of Beau's conviction. He wanted to help her despite her information source being a ghost when he could have simply dismissed her altogether.

"Okay. Okay. I'm sorry," she said. "I am judging you. But cut me a little slack—we've been on opposing sides for several years. It's not easy to just flip a switch and suddenly trust everything you do."

If she was honest with herself, she'd have to admit that her anger flares were partly an attempt to distance herself from Beau because the urge to run toward him was alarmingly strong.

He tilted his head to one side. "You trust me enough to want to kiss me."

"Lust and desire don't require trust. They only require hormones."

"Oh, I think it's more than that, counselor," Beau said. "If your attraction to me was purely physical, you would've flirted with me on the golf course or in the courthouse. Instead, I only just today became someone you would consider taking the next step with because you've started to know me and trust me." He lifted a hand up before she could protest. "Not entirely. But more than you ever did in the courtroom."

"I concede that I do trust you some. So, I'm going to trust you to have your investigator retrieve the notebook."

She trusted him. And she needed his help.

Ten

Beau drove Jenny out of the neighborhood and parked at a gas station. He didn't want to linger near the DA's house and risk being spotted by nosy neighbors. He texted Matt and waited for the call back.

During the drive, Jenny had spent the ride bickering with her ghost. He could follow most of their conversation even though he could only hear one side. Apparently, Cecilia was giving her both valuable information—Stu's garage door code and the location of the notebook—and some irrelevant, like the hemorrhoid cream in his bathroom drawer. Eventually, with frequent redirecting, Jenny seemed to be able to extract all the information she needed.

The conversation was bizarre, and yet, somehow almost believable.

When Matt called, Beau put him on speaker phone.

"You were unusually cryptic in your text, Beau. Retrieval. That's your code for B and E."

"That's right. I have assistant DA Jenny Wiley on the

line. She's going to fill you in. She doesn't know your name or identity."

Jenny shifted in the passenger seat. Because she was about to give instructions to a man to break into the house of her superior, she was bound to be nervous. And the instructions had been given to her by a ghost, no less.

But there was simply no other way to get that notebook. Together, Beau and Jenny had discussed the pros and cons of several ideas and scenarios. Even if they managed to deliver news of its hidden location through some sort of anonymous tip, it wouldn't be enough to justify a warrant to search the district attorney's home.

Jenny rattled off the address to Stu's house. "The notebook we need is located in his home office in a hidden compartment beneath his office desk. An unseen drawer."

"That's fairly specific." Matt's voice was calm, almost casual, considering crime he'd soon commit. "Man like that's got a security system. Probably not one I can bypass in a single night. If you want the job done tonight, it won't be stealthy. What's the deadline?"

"Tonight he'll be out on a dinner date. Tomorrow night he'll be at a dinner function. Sooner is better," Jenny said.

Matt grunted. "I'll need to calculate police response time at his house once the alarm is triggered. If the notebook is exactly where you said and I don't have to look around for it, I might be able to get in and out before the men in blue arrive. What about family at his home? Wife? kids?"

"Divorced—a couple of times. Kids live with their mothers," Jenny said. "As for the police, you won't have to cut it so close. I'll give you the code to Stu's garage door. That'll get you in the house from the connecting door."

Beau could feel the skepticism in Matt's silence.

"This is legit," Beau said. "And in the interest of stopping a criminal and freeing an innocent man. I wouldn't hire you for this if it wasn't important."

When Matt huffed in consent, Jenny continued, "The neighborhood houses are all located on generous sized lots, meaning they are spaced far enough apart, I doubt anyone will hear the garage door open. He has exterior security cameras, so you'll be on video and should plan accordingly."

Matt let out a low, admiring whistle. "She's crafty," he told Beau. "And handy for a job like this."

Beau winked at Jenny. "She's something special."

"Out of your league, am I right?" Matt chuckled at himself.

"You're probably right," Beau admitted.

"After the job is done, where do I bring the notebook?" Matt asked.

"My place." Beau and Jenny said simultaneously.

Jenny repeated, "My place." She turned toward Beau. "You need to never lay hands on that notebook. You're Karl's representing lawyer. I can discover it and turn it in anonymously." She turned back to the phone. "Matt, that means you need to drop it off at my place without me ever seeing you. I need to be able to honestly say I've never met the person who delivered that notebook to my doorstep."

"Her place," Beau confirmed to Matt. "Thanks."

He disconnected the call and pointed a finger at Jenny. "But you shouldn't be alone tonight. You have a head injury." When she started to protest, but he pushed on, "Do we need to have this discussion again about how you should be monitored?"

"I'll be fine. I don't need a babysitter. We'll get my car, and I'll go straight home."

Beau scowled. "We should stick together."

"For twenty-four hours? Stu knows the notebook is safely hidden in his house and doesn't know we're conspiring to take it back. I'm not in any danger. And I do have to work tomorrow. Real work—not just keeping up pretenses."

Beau frowned, debating whether or not he wanted to continue arguing. He felt uncomfortable leaving her and started to formulate a new tactic to dispute the safety of Jenny staying alone when his phone rang.

"Hi, Travis. What's up?"

"I've been in an accident. Can you come?"

Beau's heart thudded at the sound of terror in Travis's voice.

"Are you hurt? Where are you?"

"I'm okay. Just a fender bender. The police are on their way."

"Text me your address. I'll be right there."

Beau's jaw tensed. As his death grip on the steering wheel tightened, he pulled out of the parking lot and drove toward Travis.

"I need to make a detour. Travis has been in a fender bender. We'll get your car after."

"Of course," Jenny said.

Travis had said he wasn't injured, but Beau would worry until he saw Travis with his own eyes. The boy's voice had sounded shaky, but that was common after one's very first accident and didn't automatically mean there was an injury involved.

WHEN BEAU ARRIVED, the police were already on the scene, and the cars had been moved off to the right-hand lane to keep from obstructing traffic. The front right of Travis's Honda Accord was dented inward. The Jaguar parked behind had a dented front fender.

The police officer talked to the excited driver of the other vehicle, a tall man in a suit, about mid-fifties.

Beau approached a wide-eyed, sweating Travis. The boy was obviously frightened. Beau didn't know if that was because he was responsible for the accident, worried about the consequences to his driving record, or feared Beau's anger. Perhaps some combination of all of them. Beau wrapped his arms around his son to let him know he wasn't angry with him and felt some of the tension ease.

"You're not hurt?" he asked again.

Jenny stepped out of the car and inspected the crime scene.

"I'm okay," Travis said.

Beau stepped back from the hug, keeping his hands on Travis's shoulders. "What happened?"

"He ran the stop sign." Travis ran a hand through his hair. "I mean, I know I should've hesitated longer and made sure he was going to stop. I didn't expect him to drive right through it."

The police officer approached them. "Are you his father?"

"Yes," Beau said, dropping his hands.

"Mr. Avery says your son ran a stop sign." The uniformed man held an electronic pad in his hand, looking ready to issue a citation.

Beau believed Travis, but who was a police officer more likely to believe—a young, green driver or a wealthy businessman?

"Were there any witnesses?" Beau asked.

"No," the officer replied.

Jenny approached. "Officer McKenzie." She led with a smile. "Would you be Victor McKenzie's son? The homicide detective? I'm assistant district attorney Jenny Wiley. I've worked with your dad on cases." She extended her hand.

The officer's expression softened at the recognition of his father's name. He shook her hand. "Yes ma'am. I know your name. Dad calls you Wiley Coyote."

Jenny chuckled. "He's a good man. We've closed cases together." She gestured around the scene. "Wow. This brings back memories of my traffic work before homicide. I was checking out the front-end damage of the cars and the tire tracks—old habits, you know." Her voice was warm and congenial. "The damage suggests Travis's Accord was hit at an angle with the front of the Jaguar. The pattern of impact suggests that Mr. Avery is at fault. I know you probably already noticed that, but I haven't been on the traffic accident beat for a while. I guess once you learn the detective work, you never stop. Anyway, I'll let you get back to your job."

Officer McKenzie appeared to take her words to heart as he inspected the two different vehicles. Beau, Travis, and

Jenny hung back as the officer walked back over to Mr. Avery and explained the discrepancies in the damage to the cars as compared to Mr. Avery's story.

"That's a load of crap." The man raised his voice in agitation. "How long have you been out of cop school? A week?"

The young officer probably was fairly new at his job, but the businessman made a wrong move in insulting him.

McKenzie's ears reddened. "Perhaps what we should do, Mr. Avery, is a walk test and breath analysis after running a stop sign."

The man backed down. "No, no. That won't be necessary. I missed the stop sign. You see, it's not well placed, and the tree branch is obscuring it from view. We'll exchange insurance information, and I'll take care of the damage."

The officer began writing a ticket.

Beau wanted to kiss Jenny, not just because she'd saved Travis from a ticket but because of the way she'd played quiet hero without hesitation.

"WHY DON'T I drive the Accord back to your house?" Jenny offered to Beau. "Travis shouldn't drive so soon after an accident. And, yes, my head is fine." She wanted to curl in a ball in a dark room and rest.

Travis handed over the keys before Beau could reply.

"I appreciate that," Beau said.

She climbed in the car, feeling steady, and entered Beau's address into her phone GPS. After a whirlwind day of being hit on the head, telling Beau she could see ghosts, and then plotting a burglary, she needed time alone to process everything in the safety and seclusion of her own apartment. More than ever, she wished her father was alive to give her advice. If this theft plan backfired, she wouldn't just lose her job, she could end up on the wrong side of the courtroom.

She parked Travis's car outside Beau's garage and cued up a rideshare to meet her there to drive her to pick up her car.

She was climbing into the ride share when Beau pulled into the driveway.

He parked and hopped out of his car. "You're leaving?"

"Yes. I'm exhausted, and you have Travis to look after."

"I'll see you tomorrow?"

"Yes, after I turn the book in." She lowered herself into the back seat of her ride share.

"Wait." Beau gripped the car door. "Thank you for what you did for Travis back there."

He looked like he wanted to hug her, but if she gave in to that comfort now, she wouldn't leave.

With a slight shrug, she smiled faintly. "You know me. I'm all about truth and justice."

"Thank you," he repeated.

When he stepped back, she pulled the door closed.

JENNY PICKED up her car from the cemetery and drove home to the quiet stillness of her apartment. She locked her door, bolted it, and flipped the fin lock shut. Every creak in the hallway sounded like a faceless man coming to knock down her door. Maybe she didn't feel as safe as she let on to Beau.

Her head throbbed from the overwhelming events of the day. Her superior was a criminal, her courtroom enemy was turning into her romantic fantasy, and she was seeing ghosts.

After walking to the kitchen for a glass of water, she briefly considered having a glass of wine, but that was probably a bad idea since she was dehydrated and had been hit on the head earlier.

She eyed the bottle of Childress Vineyard Merlot she kept on the counter. She and her father enjoyed the brand during meals after a long, leisurely day of golf together. She'd never opened this particular bottle and knew she never would. There was too much sentimental value in that single bottle of wine.

"Cecilia? Are you here?"

No answer.

The ghost had disappeared after they'd formulated their plan for the theft with Beau's private investigator. Had Cecilia moved on?

Her father had told her spirits often lingered until their purpose with the living was fulfilled. Perhaps Cecilia's was.

Jenny showered, dressed in pajamas, and brushed and dried her hair. She gingerly touched the lump on the back of her head when her phone rang.

After answering, she put it on speaker. "Hi, sis."

"Wow, so much exhaustion built into those two words," Phoenix said.

"It's been a long day." Jenny went to her kitchen and opened the refrigerator. Sniffing at leftover chicken marsala, she decided it hadn't expired, put it on a plate, and set it in the microwave to heat it.

"Oh, yeah? I bet I have you beat."

"Did you follow a ghost to a crypt only to be hit on the head by a mugger, rescued by your arch nemesis, and nearly kiss him in his kitchen?"

"Oh, you have me beat. So, you almost kissed Beau?"

Jenny punched start on the microwave. "That's what you want to ask me about? Not my head injury?"

"You're coherent enough for a phone conversation and admitting to almost kissing a man. How bad can it be?"

"Good point. I really wanted to kiss him though. Isn't that indicative of severe head trauma?"

"Um, no. Nice try. Seriously though, are you okay?" Phoenix asked.

"Aside from the lump on my head and confessing to him about seeing ghosts, I'm a picture of health."

Phoenix gasped. "You told him?"

"I was forced to explain a series of bizarre behaviors on my part. And because our almost-kiss predated me revealing my ghost secret, actual kissing may not be in our future."

"Oh, I'm sorry. Maybe he'll come around." Phoenix's voice held no optimism.

Jenny pulled the chicken out of the microwave. "I'm going to eat dinner and watch an episode of *Alias*. Can I call you later?"

"Absolutely."

Jenny sat at the kitchen table and pushed the food around on her plate. Tomorrow, she'd have the notebook. Yet even when she turned in the evidence, her safety wasn't guaranteed. If Stu was crazed enough to commit murder, he was vindictive enough to seek revenge.

And with the notebook in police custody, she would have fulfilled her agreement to help Karl. He would be free, justice would be fulfilled, and Beau would have no further use for her. Her interactions with him would be concluded —until the next time they faced each other in courtroom.

Eleven

After Beau parked the cars in the garage, he went inside, took off his tie, and undid the top button of his shirt. Dirt marred it from helping Jenny up from the ground in the cemetery and sitting on the bench with her.

He wished she hadn't rushed off from his place. He couldn't tell if she wanted space or thought he didn't want to be around someone claiming to see ghosts. Perhaps both.

He made a mental note to text her before bed to make sure she was okay after the attack and injury.

After a quick shower, he dressed in shorts and a T-shirt.

In the kitchen, he reheated leftover lasagna and set the table for himself and Travis. They sat down across from each other, Travis looking sullen.

"I'm really sorry about the car," Travis said.

"I'm just glad you're okay. I'm not upset. It's a good lesson in defensive driving."

"Your friend got me out of a tough spot."

"She was pretty amazing, wasn't she?"

Beau had been astounded by Jenny's behavior and shocked at the generosity of it. She didn't have to say anything. She could have sat in his car and let events unfold. The traffic cop would have ticketed Travis because the young officer felt pressured from a wealthy, older citizen.

Instead, Jenny recognized what was happening and offered her unsolicited assistance while expecting nothing in return. She truly did have all the virtues of that coin she carried around: courage, wisdom, justice, and temperance. He'd seen some lawyers pretend justice in the courtroom. Jenny embodied it.

"Beau?"

He blinked. "Sorry. Did you say something?"

Travis chuckled. "I asked you if I could still drive the car to school tomorrow. But now I want to know if you're planning to date Miss Wiley."

Smiling faintly, Beau pushed the lasagna around on his plate. "I'm thinking about it."

He'd actually been trying to date Jenny for a few days now—that elusive Greek dinner they hadn't managed to have yet. It wouldn't happen until the matter of the notebook was resolved.

Maybe postponing the date a few days away was better. Beau needed time to digest everything she'd told him about interacting with Cecilia's ghost. They needed to discuss the issue further. He didn't believe in ghosts, but nor did he believe Jenny was crazy or delusional and he'd seen his share of these traits as a defense attorney.

And, yet, he had no rational explanation for the things Jenny knew.

~

THE NEXT DAY, Jenny worked in her office behind a closed door. She didn't want any surprise visitors, so when Cecilia popped into her workspace, she asked the ghost to keep an eye on Stu's activities. He'd apparently called in to say he was working from home.

Jenny typed away at a never-ending mound of paperwork and answered her revolving door of emails. She avoided coffee and sugar. Her nerves were already frayed from the long wait for sunset when Beau's man would steal the notebook back from Stu.

Cecilia had graced Jenny with hours of solitude. In fact, Jenny started to wonder again if the ghost had moved on. Karl's case was nowhere near wrapped up, but they had a solid plan on how to finagle getting the notebook into discovery, so perhaps this was sufficient enough for the apparition to transition from the living world to the afterlife.

Was there an afterlife? Somewhere calm and peaceful where no terrifying assaults happened when you stepped out of a crypt?

Jenny's thoughts drifted to Beau, who'd so far seemed to accept her claim to see Cecilia's ghost with guarded reservation rather than frightened dismay or incredulous disbelief. Would his attitude shift to more skepticism and avoidance when he had time to consider the preposterousness of her ability to see and converse with ghosts? Would he ultimately reject the possibility of a parallel paranormal world?

"That jerk!"

Jenny practically jumped out of her skin at Cecilia's sudden outburst and appearance.

"What's wrong?" Jenny asked, worried the ghost had discovered something that had unraveled their plan to get the notebook back.

"Stu is using my notebooks to start laying the groundwork for his own payoffs," Cecilia snapped.

Jenny glowered at the apparition and forced calm into her voice. "Cecilia—" she addressed the ghost as she would a child amidst a temper tantrum, "—Stu is probably going to jail later this week. If not for your murder then at least for whatever dirty deeds are detailed in your book. But that won't happen if you scare me into a heart attack."

Rather than apologize, Cecilia smacked gum and crossed her arms.

"Try to focus on the big picture," Jenny added. "The only thing blackmail will do for Stu is make more enemies." She wanted to add *and possibly get him killed,* but that seemed too harsh under Cecilia's circumstances. "When we get the notebook back and expose him, he's going to wish he'd made friends instead of enemies."

"Fine. That makes sense." Cecilia pouted. "Makes me feel a little better, too."

Jenny strummed her fingers on her desk and cleared her throat. She'd spent all morning wondering if today would be the day he decided she was too strange to touch, much less to kiss.

"How's Beau doing?" she asked.

At the arched-eyebrow expression Cecilia gave her, Jenny immediately regretted asking.

"Why?" Cecilia laughed. "You want me to pass a note to him in class? *Do you like me? Check yes or no.*"

BEAU SPENT the long hours of the day in his office reviewing Karl's case. He had the files pulled up on two large-screen monitors so he could simultaneously review police reports and crime scene photographs.

By nearly two p.m., he surrendered to his impulse and called Jenny.

"How are you?" he asked, standing and stretching.

"I think I'm losing vision in my left eye. One-sided paralysis is normal after a head injury though, right?"

"What?"

"Kidding. Just kidding. I'm fine."

"That isn't remotely funny." He managed to keep the humor out of his voice, though he liked that she felt comfortable enough to tease him.

"How is the police report analysis coming?" she asked.

"The neighbor claimed the victim was arguing with her brother. The spat was audible through the apartment wall. So, the neighbor didn't have direct visualization and assumed it was Karl. The neighbor heard a man and a woman arguing but not the specifics of what they were arguing about." Beau paced his large office near the window overlooking the city of Charlotte. The Montrose Law Offices occupied the entire floor of the building. He employed three lawyers, four paralegals, and three office assistants, with plans to hire more staff in the next year.

Jenny said, "Which means those voices could've been

Cecilia and Stu, Cecilia and her brother, or Cecilia and a plumber. Honestly, all the neighbor knew was a man and a woman were arguing."

Beau rolled his shoulders, feeling the familiar ache between his shoulder blades where tension typically settled. "Right. There was no forced entry, and the crime didn't take place immediately inside Cecilia's living room, which would've been the location closest to the door. The murder happened in the kitchen."

"So she was arguing with a man she obviously knew and let inside her apartment, and the bickering moved into the kitchen where it escalated."

Beau continued, "The argument culminated there and the right combination of motive, madness, and murder weapon resulted in Cecilia being stabbed. Twice."

"Anything about the injuries that could be helpful?"

"According to the coroner's report, there were two different stab wounds—the initial wound and then the lethal wound. The initial wound was calculated to be made with both the victim and the assailant in standing positions. Based on the downward trajectory of the blade and rib markings, the coroner gave a height of the attacker at five ten. Right-handed. Karl is five nine, but the prosecuting attorney would argue that the coroner height estimation was just that—an estimate."

"And both Stu and Karl are right-handed. I wouldn't be surprised if half the names in Cecilia's notebook fit that description."

His office phone rang, and he tapped the intercom.

"Your two o'clock is here," his assistant said.

"Give me five minutes. Thanks." He put his phone

back up to his ear. "I have to go. I'll see you tonight? Greek dinner." He didn't want to wait until tonight to see her, but events had to unfold as planned.

"After the notebook."

"After the notebook, text me and we'll meet up."

"Okay."

The conclusions from their discussion of the crime scene were grim, but Beau enjoyed discussing the case with Jenny. Working a problem with her felt less like opposing counsel and more like a partnership he hadn't realized he wanted.

Stu drank scotch on the rocks as he socialized with Charlotte's high-class citizens at Sophia's Lounge—named for Queen Sophia Charlotte, the wife of England's King George III. The opulent location was set inside the Ivey's Hotel.

He didn't typically drink hard liquor at these events because he didn't want to be disinhibited and say or do anything he might later regret. His reputation mattered. Normally, he drank red wine while socializing, but he hadn't been able to consume anything crimson-colored since the murder. It looked too much like blood. Too much like the stains that sometimes blotched his hands.

Staring up at the luxurious chandelier, his mind wandered to recent events. He was still furious at Cecilia forcing his hand. His actions had been a form of self-defense, self-preservation. He'd dedicated his life to helping this community. He put criminals behind bars. Then, a hooker had threatened to dismantle his life's work with petty blackmail.

When his phone buzzed, he pulled it from his pocket and glanced at the notification. His home alarm system had detected movement in front of one of the exterior cameras. It was probably that damn skunk who kept prowling near his garage after dark, but he opened the video footage to double check.

A man entered the camera's view, wearing a hoodie and keeping his face away from the camera lens. Then the intruder punched in the key code to the garage door.

It opened.

Stu's mouth dropped open. Impossible.

The phone app gave Stu the option to call the police with a single tap of a button. They'd be at his house in under five minutes and intercept the burglar.

But he hesitated. What would police find? A burglar attempting to steal his electronics, watches, and cash? Or someone specifically targeting the notebook? And if the thief was arrested, notebook in hand, the evidence would go straight into police custody.

No. He couldn't allow that.

But someone stealing the notebook was inconceivable. No one knew about the existence of the notebook except Jenny, and she didn't know Stu had it. Or did she? Wiley Coyote had an unsettling ability to know things about cases.

His thumb hovered over the screen. He couldn't take the chance that this break-in was connected to the notebook. Deciding not to alert the police, Stu pressed the decline button.

Without bothering to say goodbye to anyone at the party, he dropped his emptied glass on the bar counter, turned on his heels, and left.

He tried to assure himself he was being paranoid; the presence of the burglar was probably unrelated to the notebook. Even as he tempered his worry, he began forming plans for retaliation against Jenny. And since Beau was the one who'd enlisted her help with the case, Stu may need to silence them both, simultaneously.

As he walked to his car, splotchy red spots bloomed across his hand. Sweat formed along his hairline and trickled down the back of his neck.

Why had Jenny meddled?

If she was after the notebook, it had to be either as evidence of Stu's illegal activities or something that would make him appear suspect in Cecilia's death—or both.

Jenny was forcing his hand just as Cecilia had.

The people now threatening to unravel his life had to be stopped. Beau was worse than Cecilia because he gave the threat teeth. And Jenny... Jenny had defiled his respect and his office's loyalty. Her betrayal cut deeper than blackmail had.

BEAU DROVE HOME FROM WORK, using the quiet car ride to sort through his thoughts and tangled emotions. He didn't like leaving Jenny alone last night or all day today, not so soon after she'd been attacked. But his discomfort was emotional rather than logical. As she'd pointed out, she didn't need him right now.

Jenny's claim to see Cecilia's ghost was positively mind-boggling. Ghosts didn't exist. They couldn't exist. Right?

Yet, Jenny couldn't have known the things she knew without tremendous inside information. Even if she had a living informant who'd told her the location of the notebook at the crypt, nothing explained how she knew DA Winslow's garage door code or where he'd hidden the book. Could she have already known the code—perhaps learned it some other way? But for the sake of her own credibility, Jenny would have provided Beau with a logical explanation and not created a paranormal one.

Then, she'd produced information about his family reunion twenty years ago. That entire exchange had been surreal.

Tonight, if Matt found the notebook exactly where Jenny said it would be, Beau might be forced to accept Jenny's spiritual connections. She'd been with Beau during the day yesterday from the time the notebook was stolen to when she told Matt where it was hidden at Stu's; therefore, she couldn't have discovered the location without Beau knowing how she'd done it. She'd briefly been in his bathroom alone, but she'd left her phone sticking out of the side pocket of her purse in his car at the time.

And amidst all of yesterday afternoon's bizarre activities, Beau had nearly kissed Jenny. When he'd mentioned the kiss later, she hadn't denied the moment and hadn't refuted wanting to kiss him also. Maybe he had something to look forward to when the issue of this notebook was resolved.

After pulling into his garage, he parked the car.

Travis met him at the door with his backpack slung over

one shoulder, a pizza box in one hand, and a slice of meat-lovers in the other.

He chewed and swallowed a bite. "Hey, I was just heading over to Monty's to work on our science project."

"Yeah, I saw your text. Thanks for letting me know. I couldn't text back while driving. You'll be back before nine?"

"Yes, sir."

"Okay. I'm having dinner with Jenny this evening."

Travis raised his eyebrows with a goofy grin. "Don't wait up for you?"

"Very funny. It's not like that."

Not yet anyway, Beau thought.

Travis took another bite of pizza and headed out the door to walk through the neighborhood to his friend's house.

Beau dropped his briefcase off in his home office. He still had work to do, but it could wait until after a shower.

Hopefully, by the time he finished and the sun set, Jenny would have turned in the notebook. He'd feel better once that ticking time bomb book of secrets was locked in a police evidence room. And when Stu Winslow was locked behind bars, assuming there was enough evidence to lead to the arrest of Stu Winslow, Beau could finally stop worrying about who would be targeted next.

After showering and slipping into a comfortable pair of blue jeans and a t-shirt, Beau entered his home office. He planned to work for a few minutes until he heard from Jenny. A dozen resumes awaited review for potential new hires at his law firm, and he hoped the task would take his mind off the restless tension of waiting.

The doorbell rang.

He walked down the hall toward the front entrance. "Travis, did you forget your house key again?"

When Beau unbolted and opened the door, he startled at the snarling face of Stu Winslow and the dark shape clutched in his hand.

Beau's instinct was to slam the door shut, but Stu threw his weight into the door, forcing it open and knocking Beau backward. Stu had the element of surprise, but Beau was no lightweight to be pushed around.

He regained his balance and raised his fists, preparing to fight.

Stu fired his weapon.

Twelve

Jenny arrived back at her apartment, parked her car in her designated space, and took the stairs up to her third-floor apartment.

Once inside, she changed out of her business suit and into comfortable black cotton slacks and a green cotton shirt. She brushed her long hair down and loose as she considered how to busy herself until the package arrived.

A knock sounded at her door.

Special delivery!

Jenny rushed over and checked the peephole. A shadow retreated from the doorway.

Angst pummeled her stomach. In a low voice to herself, she said, "Please be the notebook. Please be the notebook."

She gave Beau's man another thirty seconds to vacate the premises.

After unlocking and opening the door, she stared down at the notebook on the floor with some mixture of elation and dread. "Oh. It's like Christmas," she murmured to herself. She picked it up, feeling the oppressive weight of it. "If I was given coal, but really needed to start a fire."

With sweating palms, she closed and bolted her door before slipping on a pair of flats and grabbing her keys.

Cecilia appeared, blocking the doorway.

Jenny sucked in a sharp breath and clutched her chest. "You scared me! You've got to stop doing that."

"It's not my fault you're so skittish."

Jenny suppressed the urge to remind Cecilia she was still flesh and blood, and a killer was on the loose. "Never mind." She waved the notebook at the ghost. "We have it."

Cecilia frowned. "Not for long."

Fear prickled along Jenny's spine. "What does that mean?" She didn't like Cecilia's solemn tone.

"Stu's stooge—the one who hit you in the cemetery—is here."

"What? Why didn't you lead with that?" Jenny's heart raced, knocking against her chest harder than a judge's gavel rapping against an anvil during courtroom chaos. "Can I make it to my car?"

"No." Cecilia's expression looked desolate and full of pity.

Jenny's mouth went dry. Was her outlook so bleak?

A hired man. He wouldn't make the mistake of leaving her alive this time. Except, he wouldn't get the drop on her this time either.

Tightening her grip on the notebook, she scanned the apartment for a weapon. She didn't cave in the courtroom under pressure, and she certainly wouldn't cower from an attacker in her own home.

"He thinks he's going to take me down? We'll see about that."

"Call the police," Cecilia suggested.

"They won't get here in time before he breaks in." By the time police arrived, Jenny would be a corpse, and the notebook would be gone.

She searched her kitchen for something heavy. If she had a proper house with a fireplace, she'd own a poker stick —perfect for striking. After all, every good murder mystery series put a poker stick to good use.

"What about the balcony?" Cecilia asked.

"I'm three stories up. I'll break a leg."

"Put the door chain up," Cecilia said.

"No." Jenny squared her shoulders. "He has to break inside thinking I don't know he's here."

Her gaze fell on the unopened bottle of Merlot on the counter, one of the last gifts her father had given her.

"Thanks, Dad." Snatching the bottle, she dashed for the bathroom down the hall.

She leaned inside, turned on the shower, and pulled the palm tree decorative curtain shut.

"You're taking a shower?"

Jenny rolled her eyes. "For someone who was smart enough to keep secrets in life, you're not putting two and two together in death."

Jenny turned on her sound system, and Jennifer Lopez sang *Jenny from the Block*.

Cecilia gaped at her.

"Don't judge me. My dad loved Jennifer Lopez. And even Abe Lincoln loved music. '*Listening to melody*,' he once said, '*man ... measures the depths of his own nature.*'"

"Didn't he die outside an opera house?"

"It was a play at a theatre."

"Close enough," Cecilia retorted.

Jenny waved the wine bottle at the ghost in frustration. "Keep quiet, but let me know when the intruder is close." She packed her purse, notebook, and keys into a satchel and slung it diagonally across her chest.

"You're laying a trap," Cecilia finally deduced, sounding half impressed, half horrified.

"I hope so," Jenny said.

"And the twenty year-old song is so he thinks you can't hear him coming."

"That, and to cover up the sound of me hyperventilating." And her racing heart, which was beating so loudly the neighbors could probably hear it.

"He's picking the lock of your door," Cecilia whispered.

Jenny hid just inside her darkened bedroom—out of sight from the hallway and the path Stu's man would take on his way to the running shower.

She wanted to ask the spirit what was the point of whispering when only Jenny could hear her, but she suspected Cecilia's lowered voice was a reflection of her genuine worry for Jenny's safety.

"Hallway," Cecilia said.

If Jenny didn't know better, she would've thought the ghost was holding her breath from the suspense.

Jenny tightened her grip on the bottle, palms slick, and tried to decide which swing she would use. Down like an ax? Sideways like a baseball bat? Up like a ... up like a golf swing. Yes. Rotate the hips.

One good hit. Then out the door, down the stairs, and into her car before the intruder had a chance to retaliate.

A shadow passed the doorway, and Jenny's knees turned watery.

Give me courage, Dad.

Her hands shook so badly she was afraid she'd drop the bottle. She tightened her grip until her knuckles ached and stepped into the hall anyway.

And swung.

BEAU BLINKED his eyes open to a pair of black dress shoes. He was lying on the floor of his foyer. His mouth was dry and his muscles ached.

When the Taser had hit him, every nerve in his body seared with agony as he went rigid and fell to the floor. The pain built with a crescendo until stopping abruptly. Now his nerves felt cooked to a crisp.

When he started to stir, he felt the constraints on his hands. He looked down at the electrical tape wound tightly around his wrists bound in front of him.

His gaze lifted to the intruder standing over him. "Stu."

"Where's the notebook, Beau?" the DA demanded, smoothing the front of his tuxedo.

Tension in Beau's chest eased slightly at the question. If the man didn't have the notebook, then he didn't have Jenny. At least, not yet. Stu had still gotten the drop on Beau, and that shouldn't have happened.

"Can I get off the floor so we can discuss this?" Beau asked.

"My plan wasn't really to interrogate you down there. But you're heavier than you look. Two hundred? Two twenty?"

"One ninety."

"Oh yeah? What do you do? Weigh yourselves after four hours of golf, sweating off ten pounds?"

Beau had no intention of discussing weight with the crazed district attorney waving a Taser at him.

Beau shifted, pushing himself up to a seated position.

Stu jolted, as if expecting an attack. Apparently, he'd never been hit with a Taser or he'd know the body didn't immediately cooperate after being electrocuted.

"Easy. I'm just sitting up," Beau said, holding his taped hands out to remind Stu he was tied. "Can I move to a chair so we can have this conversation like two civilized people?"

Stu scowled but jerked his head in the direction of the dining room. Beau stood slowly, not wanting to alarm him. And he certainly didn't want to get hit with bolts of electricity again. He could tackle the other attorney, but there was no guarantee a hit would knock that torture device out of Stu's hand.

"I'm not the villain here, you know." Still holding the Taser in one hand, Stu rubbed irritably at the palm of his left hand as if something sticky clung to it.

"By all means, enlighten me." Beau refrained from pointing out that he was the one tied up, and Stu the one brandishing a weapon. Beau needed to stall and think of a way out of his captivity.

"Jenny forced my hand by finding that notebook. You're the one who dragged her into this."

"You had possession of the notebook. Why didn't you just destroy it?"

Stu scoffed. "Do you have any idea what a gold mine that piece of junk is? There's material on dirty cops, judges, politicians, and business owners."

"And you." Beau had no idea what was in the notebook; he hadn't even laid eyes on the cursed thing.

"And you?" Stu countered. "I haven't had a chance to go through it page by page, but there must be something juicy because you want it so badly. What dirt did the hooker pick up on the famous, smooth-talking Beaufort Montrose?"

Beau's temple throbbed. "Cecilia. Her name is Cecilia. She was my cousin. I want the notebook because I'm representing her brother," he reminded him. "Rumor has it the notebook reveals a lot of people with motive superseding my client, who is guilty of nothing more than wanting his sister to stop using drugs and get her life together."

Stu studied him with an expression of confusion and disbelief. Then, he asked again, "Where is the notebook?" He waved a hand above his head. "I will turn this place inside out."

"Be my guest."

Just be gone before my son gets home, Beau thought. He glanced at the clock. Eight-thirty. Travis might come home any minute and stumble straight into this nightmare.

Beau didn't dare admit to Stu that he didn't have the book—such an admission would only bring to light who did. Stu already knew Jenny had had it in her possession yesterday. If Beau didn't have it, Stu would guess she was the next likely person.

"Are you saying that because you think the is book well-hidden or because your girlfriend has it?"

Before Beau could answer, Stu continued, "I'm not above using this again—" he lifted the Taser in the air "—to motivate you to give me the information I want. I still have two more shots before needing to reload. And if you're trying to protect Jenny, don't bother. I've already contracted someone to visit her place."

Sharp icicles of fear sliced through Beau, almost like he was being shocked again.

On Stu's payroll was the other man who'd attacked Jenny at the crypt. Beau wished he and Jenny had stayed together, but neither one of them had suspected Stu would discover the missing book so quickly, and Jenny had made the valid point that Beau needed to not lay eyes on the notebook until it was logged into evidence.

For the first time since he'd dragged himself out of a juvenile record, Beau felt truly, utterly doomed.

Thirteen

J enny's wine bottle made solid contact with the back of her intruder's skull on the upswing.

With a grunt of pain, the man collapsed to the floor. The gun he'd been holding hit the linoleum with a clatter.

"Hurts, doesn't it?" She wasn't normally a vengeful person, but payback in this moment felt mildly satisfying.

She set the wine bottle down and picked up his gun, stuffing it into her purse. Then she reached into the shower and turned off the water faucet.

As she pivoted to leave the bathroom, the man lashed out a hand. Jenny screeched and jerked backward as his hand closed over her foot. When she yanked away, her foot came out of her shoe.

She sprinted down the hall and out the door.

"Is he chasing me?" she asked Cecilia through gasps of air. She scurried down the stairs.

"No. He's still on the floor."

"You didn't mention he had a gun."

"Would it've helped? Besides, he's a bad guy. Did you assume he wouldn't be armed?"

Jenny reached her car. It unlocked automatically with the key's proximity, and she practically dove inside before yanking the door shut. Cecilia appeared in the passenger seat.

Once Jenny was in drive and on the road, her breathing finally began to slow. Pulling out her phone, she dialed 9-1-1, and requested police and an ambulance at her apartment for an intruder. When she hung up, she continued to circle the block, watching her complex in the rearview mirror. Only after she spotted flashing blue lights turning into the parking lot would she park and talk to the police.

"Beau's in trouble," Cecilia uttered with a distant look in her eyes.

"What? What are you seeing?"

"Stu saw the break-in when his phone app alerted him to movement. When he came home and found the only thing missing was the notebook, he knew it was you. He sent his hired thug to your place, and he went to Beau's house himself. He's there now."

Jenny took a right at the next intersection, immediately thinking of the shortest route to Beau's house.

Motion sensors with phone alerts. *Dang*, Jenny thought. They hadn't considered that possibility.

"Is Beau hurt?" Fresh panic surged through her "Oh, God. He's got a son. Is Travis okay?"

"Travis is at a friend's house. But Stu has Beau tied up."

"Okay. Tied up is alive. Though we already know Stu is capable of murder." She glanced at Cecilia. "Sorry."

Cecilia waved a hand of dismissal.

After another turn, Jenny wrung the steering wheel with her hands. "You saved my life back there, warning me know that guy was coming."

"You're helping Karl, so we're even."

"Still. Thank you. I know we haven't exactly been cordial to each other."

The apparition shrugged. "I'm grumpy because I'm dead. You're grumpy because seeing ghosts is a life-altering phenomenon. Let's just get through this together."

"Agreed."

Jenny took a left, fighting the urge not to speed. Getting pulled over would only delay getting to Beau.

"Why didn't Stu come after me himself?" she asked. Of the two of them—her and Beau—she was the easier target.

Cecilia explained, "Based on the conversation between Stu and his hired thug, Stu thought Beau would be most likely to have it because he's Karl's attorney, and if anybody had the gumption to pay someone to break into Stu's home, it would be Beau."

Jenny debated calling the police again, this time about Beau. But what if that action triggered a stand-off? What if Beau became a hostage? Stu was desperate, and obviously irrational. But he wanted the notebook, which meant Jenny had her ticket inside Beau's house. Better for her and Cecilia to handle this without the police.

As she drove, a plan started to take shape.

FIFTEEN MINUTES LATER, Jenny stood before Beau's front door. She'd wedged the gun along her spine under the satchel strap. With her fingers linked behind her head and her back to the peephole, her pose was intended to suggest she was someone's captive. Hopefully, Stu would fall for the ruse.

She tried to make herself as large as possible in hopes the DA wouldn't notice the absence of a person in the darkness behind her.

Sweat trickled down the back of her neck, and fear knotted her stomach. Behind that door lurked an evil man. A man who had already proven he was capable of murder. A man who was desperate enough to cover his tracks by murdering again.

"What are you waiting for?" Cecilia asked.

"Courage." Jenny thought of the coin in her pocket and Abe Lincoln's words: *It often requires more courage to dare to do right than to fear to do wrong.*

"You have a real gun, and he has the stun gun thingy that fires the doohickies," Cecilia said. "What's the dilemma?"

Jenny looked back in disbelief at Cecilia. "He has a Taser? You might've mentioned that sooner."

"Didn't I?"

Jenny pursed her lips. In the history of all ghost and medium interactions, she wondered if she had the most ostentatious of them all. However, Cecilia had warned her about the man coming to Jenny's apartment and Beau's current predicament, so she'd proven useful even if her information was sometimes selective.

Cecilia leaned in and whispered words of encouragement, "Just imagine you're Jennifer Garner in *Alias* about to save the day ... and woo the man."

On the exhalation of a deep breath, Jenny rang the doorbell.

EVERY MUSCLE in Beau's body tensed when he heard the sound of the doorbell. From his angle in the dining room, he couldn't see through the small, decorative window to the other side of the front door.

Travis is home early, he thought.

Stu had maintained his composure with a single hostage, but if Travis walked in and saw his father tied up, his son would become a witness. A liability Stu couldn't afford to let live if he was going to get away with murder.

With his hands out of sight, under the table, Beau continued to work relentlessly on loosening the tape around his wrists. Sweat soaked his body and the moisture unstuck the sticky side of the glue on the electrical tape, making it slick. As it loosened, the tape gained enough elasticity that he was able to stretch it.

Stu stalked to the door and peered through the small side window panel. "Why the hell did he bring her here?" he muttered.

Her?

Beau's heart sank. Not Jenny.

Stu shifted the Taser in his left hand and yanked open the front door with his right. "Get in here, you idiot. The neighbors might see you holding a woman at gunpoint in a subdivision."

Jenny stepped into the foyer, arms held high with hands behind her head. She wore fitted pants and a cotton shirt now. Her long hair was loose, framing her face in a way

Beau had never seen. A satchel crossed her chest, and one shoe was missing.

He glanced behind her but saw no one.

Once inside, she slid three steps away from Stu and dropped her hands, producing a gun almost out of midair.

Stu flung the door shut as he took a surprised stumble backward. "How did you—?"

"Stop," Jenny said. "I called the police. We're all going to wait here calmly until they arrive."

Jenny glanced at Beau. "I told them where your son is staying and asked them to send an officer over there to make sure Travis won't come home until the scene is safe."

Relief washed over Beau. Believing her words meant stepping closer to believing in ghosts, because the only way she could know where Travis had gone—and that Beau was in trouble—was through paranormal channels.

He smiled faintly. "I could marry you right now, you know that, right?"

"I think we should have that kiss first." She gave him an adorable grin before turning her focus back on Stu.

"Yes, ma'am."

"Drop the Taser," Jenny repeated to Stu, more firmly this time.

"You realize you're pointing a gun at the district attorney of this city?" Stu sneered. "I am a respected official. I could end your career. Think about what you're doing, Jenny."

"I'm doing my job. You murdered someone, and now you need to face justice." Conviction kept her voice solid, but the gun in her hand shook slightly.

Stu bent slowly to set down his Taser, keeping his eyes trained on Jenny. "You can still fix this. I'll forgive you."

A glint of calculation flashed in Stu's eyes. Beau recognized the look of a predator assessing prey for weakness. Jenny might hold a gun, but she wouldn't fire it. Her courtroom savvy didn't translate into a kill-or-be-killed survival instinct.

Beau worked frantically to free his hands.

He admired Jenny's value in human life. It was the reason she'd agreed to help Beau with Karl's case—because she was a decent person. Beau's train of thought soberly reminded him that if anything happened to Jenny, it was his fault. He'd recruited her help.

As Stu slowly rose from lowering the Taser to the floor, he took the opportunity to pounce.

The DA sprang toward Jenny, striking her with his full weight and tackling her to the floor.

WHEN JENNY'S head struck the hardwood, pain momentarily blinded her. Air swooshed out of her lungs as Stu's weight crushed her. He was heavier than she expected, and the force of impact was like being slammed by a bear.

When she regained focus, he was still on top of her, trying to wrestle the gun from her grasp. His wild eyes and frothing mouth of fury made him look like a rabid dog.

She thought of poor Cecilia. If Stu had a knife in his possession right now, he wouldn't hesitate to plunge it into Jenny's chest the way he'd done to the other woman.

Jenny fought to maintain control of the gun, but Stu was stronger. Soon, he'd yank it free and use it against her.

Then the weight was lifted. Beau hauled Stu off Jenny and tossed him against one of the walls like a sack of potatoes.

Before Stu could recover, Beau hit him with the Taser. Stu's body locked, muscles jerking as the charge hit, then he crumpled into a twitching heap.

"Hurts, doesn't it?" Beau snapped.

Jenny was too busy catching her breath to laugh at the irony between her response to her attacker and Beau's to Stu.

Beau set the Taser aside and turned toward her, helping her stand. "You okay?"

"I think I hit the other side of my head this time. Maybe I'll have matching lumps." She touched a hand to the newest bruise. "Ow."

Sirens wailed in the distance.

"The notebook is safe?"

She patted her satchel.

"And Cecilia told you I was in trouble?"

"She told me I was in trouble first. Once we dealt with my attacker, we came up with a plan to rescue you. Turns out, having a ghost watching your back is handy."

Beau pulled her into his arms and wrapped her in a tight embrace. "You're amazing. Thank you."

Fourteen

Jenny sank onto her couch, exhaustion pressing down like a heavy blanket. The silence in her apartment felt almost unreal after forty-eight hours of running, fighting, panicking, and saving a life.

The police had arrived at Beau's house and arrested Stu Winslow. It was too soon to know if a case could be made to charge him with Cecilia's murder, but he would be charged with assault on Beau regardless. At some point, the Superior Court would likely remove him from his position.

Stu's hired thug was behind bars, charged with burglary from breaking into Jenny's apartment.

Jenny had spent the night following the attacks and the subsequent day answering police questions and completing paperwork. She maintained that the notebook had arrived anonymously, and when she'd gone to Beau's house, she stumbled upon Stu there.

Once home, she updated Phoenix on events and collapsed into sleep.

The next day, she'd taken off work. Beau had texted her

repeatedly, checking in on her and making sure she was physically and emotionally well. She'd reassured him repeatedly. He finished off the text message chain by inviting her over to his house for Greek takeout tomorrow—the dinner they'd yet to share.

Cecilia appeared, this time slowly shimmering into view on the couch beside Jenny.

"You're still here," Jenny said.

Cecilia shrugged, her aura heavy with a dim melancholy. "You've been kinda busy."

"You saved my life and Beau's life," Jenny said, hoping to cheer her up.

"You saved Karl's."

"We've all won." Jenny smiled. "I think this is the part where you get to move on. Despite our differences, I'll miss you, Cecilia Dixon."

"I led a terrible life." She fidgeted with her acrylic nails.

"That's not true. You led a *troubled* life. Sometimes we take the wrong path."

Cecilia continued to pout.

"Look at what you did with your second chance. You redeemed yourself by helping your brother. And you saved the two people helping him."

The ghost sniffed. "I guess so."

"I know so. Karl would be proud of how you helped."

Cecilia lifted her head and looked into Jenny's face. Finally, a smile spread across her red lips. "Yeah, he would." She swallowed and nodded. "Okay. I'm ready to go. Take care of yourself, counselor. And ... enjoy Beau. The man looks at you like you hung the moon."

Cecilia's ghostly form brightened around the edges

before vanishing entirely. Jenny felt a surprising ache tug at her chest. For all their sniping, the ghost had been her ally, her witness, and her unexpected friend.

Although this ghost had vanished, Jenny had to accept that her life with paranormal interactions beyond her father's coin was real, unpredictable, and far from over.

JENNY STOOD outside Beau's front door. The emotions swirling through her felt very different from the fear she'd experienced the last time she was here. A different type of fear had her hesitating.

She wore jeans and a shimmering red chemise ready for ... was it a date? So much had happened since their almost-kiss on Monday. Now that she and Beau were out of danger and spent a few days apart, he would have had time to process her ghostly interactions. He might decide he wanted nothing further to do with her.

She reached for another Abe quote from memory.

"The best way to predict your future, is to create it."

She rang the doorbell.

Beau opened the door looking both casual and spectacular in a pair of blue jeans and a light blue Polo shirt. He smiled at her. "Welcome back. I see you have two shoes on this time."

"Nice to see you're not tied up on the floor," she quipped back.

"I'm lucky a special woman came to my rescue. Come in." He motioned for her to enter.

Jenny stepped inside, and Beau closed the door.

"Oh? She must've thought you were worth saving." She set her purse down on a small table in his foyer.

"I'm glad she did. She's the most remarkable woman I know."

Heat crept into Jenny's cheeks as she followed him to the kitchen table. Greek takeout was already prepared on individual plates, and two red candles burned on the table. Two glasses of Agiorgitiko had been poured.

"This looks rather like a date." Her voice had an edge of excitement and hopefulness, which surprised her.

"That was the impression I was going for." He took her hand in his. "I wasn't sure you'd actually show," he admitted softly. "I'd like to date you, Jenny."

"About Cecilia—"

"You're making a believer out of me," Beau said. "I don't know how it's possible, but I don't have any other explanation. I still want to date you, paranormal activity and all." Keeping her hands in his, he scooted closer to her.

"Cecilia moved on, but you should know there will likely be others."

"I think we did pretty well with her. Come what may."

"Okay, let's begin this dinner date, shall we?" She gestured toward the food on the table.

Beau didn't move to take a seat. Instead, he pulled Jenny into his arms. "Our time together has been unpredictable. I think the next best step is to finally share that kiss we haven't yet enjoyed. Then dinner."

"That's the best idea I've heard all week." She arched up to kiss him, and the intimacy was everything she imagined it would be and more.

His lips were warm and soft. Beau deepened the kiss,

sending waves of delight all the way down to the tips of her toes.

When they broke apart, Beau was smiling. "I could get used to kisses like that. Maybe we should start all of our dinner dates like this."

"Hmm, I'm going to need a little more convincing," she teased, pressing closer.

He kissed her again, and she let the last of the fear drain away.

Whatever ghosts, trials, or chaos came next, she finally believed she wasn't facing them alone. Wrapped in his embrace, blissfully close to his body, his words echoed melodiously in her mind: *Come what may.*

<<<***>>>

***** QUICK NOTE FROM THE AUTHOR *****

READY FOR ANOTHER sweet and magical romantic suspense? There are so many delights to enjoy! Keep scrolling for the first chapter in the next book.

IN BOXED SETS

. . .

INDIVIDUAL BOOKS

Romancing the Spirit Series #1
Sadie's Spirit / Willow's Windfall
Cassie's Chase / Phoebe's Pharaoh
Vanessa's Valentine / Autumn's Angel
Romancing the Spirit Series #2
Carol's Christmas / Allison's Alibi
Gracelynn's Genie / Michelle's Miracle
Heather's Hero / Chloe's Cupid
Romancing the Spirit Series #3
Sabrina's Storm / Jenny's Justice
Stella's Star / Gigi's Gift
Phoenix's Phantom / Fiona's Freedom

THE CHRISTMAS COLLECTION

Dear Reader

If you enjoyed this book and want to know about future releases by CB Samet you can CLICK HERE to sign up for my mailing list! I promise I won't spam you. I only send an email when I have a new book released, giveaways, or special discounts. And I'll never sell your information. You can also unsubscribe at any time.

Do you enjoy paperbacks? I have an Etsy shop where you can purchase signed copies of my books.

Also, as an independent author, I rely heavily on readers to spread the word about books they've read. If you enjoyed this story, kindly let others know by posing a brief comment on social media or leave a review where you purchased it.

Keep reading for excerpts from another of my books!

Thank you for reading,
CB Samet
www.cbsamet.com

Other Books by CB Samet

The Shadow Guardians Trilogy

Urban fantasy Norse Mythology Adventure

Raven's Flight, prequel novella

Raine Down, Book 1

Rosalyn's Run, novella

Storm Surge, Book 2

Anka's Orb, novella

Sky Fall, Book 3

Olympian Awakenings Trilogy

Urban fantasy Greek Mythology Adventure

Grab the prequel exclusively HERE.

Stone Hearts / Winds of Destiny / Flame and Shadow

The Rider Files

Romantic Suspense Thrillers

Meridian File / Masters File / Box Set 1

McMillan File / Maltisse File /Box Set 2

Storm File / Sullivan File / Box Set 3

Sharp File / Sizani File / Box Set 4

Rivera File / Rucker File / Box Set 5

Richmond File / Redwood File / Box Set 6

Atlas File / Angel File / Box Set 7

Buy 4book box sets direct from author and save 10%

Payhip. Use code E152M0GZG4

~

The Dr. Whyte Adventure Novels
Thriller Series

Black Gold / Whyte Knight / Gray Horizon

Gigi's Gift

~

Gigi will need more than the luck o' the Irish to solve this haunting mystery—especially when love and lies collide.

Detective Gigi Montgomery has been suppressing her ability to see ghosts her entire life. But when her best friend's shade appears, Gigi is determined to find the culprit—and that means facing her fears of the paranormal.

Rory Dunnigan is an Irish antiquities dealer and philanthropist who finds himself romantically interested in detective Gigi Montgomery. But her investigation into her friend's assault threatens to uncover secrets of his own.

Can they find the culprit and stop the next disaster or will their secrets tear them apart?

SAMPLE CHAPTER

Sweat dripped from Rory's brow as he hung suspended above the floor, fingers brushing the priceless Irish cross. He strained to keep his weight evenly balanced in the harness around his torso. Beneath him, the ornate, ceremonial, twelve-inch cross rested atop a red velvet cushion on a pedestal in the center of a circular room filled with priceless antiquities.

Although it had been restored, the gold, silver, and copper had only a dull sheen and still bore the marks of centuries of survival—nicks, dents, and tarnished metal. The jewels had long since been distanced from the cross and traded across continents—scattered to the wind and thought forever lost to Irish heritage.

But Rory had located them through careful searching over the years. And he'd added them to his collection—some through outright buying, others more craftily. Like tonight.

"Steady. It's weighted, lad."

Rory glanced at the ghost of his distant ancestor. "*Sea*, Emmet. I'm well aware." His voice was irritable. He didn't need the ghost reminding him what he already knew in the middle of a heist. One mis-movement and Rory could set off the alarms in the vault.

He plucked the imitation cross from his waist and readied for the exchange.

"If you botch this an' the alarm's raised, the room seals, and all oxygen's evacuated." Emmet's Irish accent was thick, and he spoke faster than Rory. His shimmering form was that of an old Irishman with whitish, wiry hair, wearing a beige léine—a long linen tunic that came down to his knees

—over brown pants, and topped off with a brat—a smoke-colored, wool, sleeveless, hoodless cloak.

"Yeah, you've mentioned that already." Rory grunted with the effort of keeping himself steady in the harness.

"I suppose it's not as difficult as the ruby you stole in Bangladesh."

Rory grunted his agreement. "You neglected to tell me that the little red stone was guarded by a tiger." Quick as lightning, Rory traded out the fake cross for the authentic one.

"I see some things," Emmet defiantly puffed out his chest, "but I'm not omniscient."

Rory pressed the button on his waist, and the electronic reel pulled him up toward the ventilation duct. As he rose, he tucked the ceremonial cross in his satchel.

"Well done," Emmet congratulated him.

Rory hoisted himself into the duct work before disconnecting the harness. Thankfully, the apparatus had held his weight. He broke down the equipment and stuffed it into this backpack, and pushing the pack ahead of him in the cramped space, crawled through the maze.

He exited the way he'd entered at the basement level. Adrenaline surged through him, but he tried to temper the impulse to revel in his success. He still needed to vacate the premises without notice.

Before climbing out the window, he pulled on the backpack and wiped his brow with his sleeve.

"All clear?" he asked.

"Sound as a pound, lad," Emmet replied.

When Rory reached fresh air outside the building, Emmet squeaked out an, "Uh, oh."

Rory froze. "What uh oh?"

"A raccoon triggered the south exit route. The guards've pooled over there. You'll have to go west."

"Where the motion-sensor lights are?"

"Aye."

Rory sighed as he flexed his muscles, ready for a dash through darkness and gardens. He would have to rely on Emmet's ghostly apparition.

"Show me the way."

Gigi clinked her tall glass of lager to Lexi's. "Cheers!"

They sipped their respective beers, Gigi enjoying the thick, bitter liquid.

"Another week almost gone," Lexi said.

They met every Thursday to have drinks at O'Shaugnessy's and celebrate an end to the work-week—almost. Fridays were too crowded in the bar, so Thursday had become their celebratory day. Except, tonight was the first Thursday they'd seen each other in a month, owing to busy schedules.

"Your museum display is interfering with our Thirsty Thursdays," Gigi said lightly.

"I know, I know. It's been hectic, but it'll get better. We're cataloging display pieces on loan from a private collector. Once I catch up, the hours will go back to normal." Lexi's gaze followed a man walking through the bar.

"And it's probably interfering with your love life," Gigi

added, watching her friend scan the room like a feline predator on the hunt.

Lexi had full lips and long, wavy brown hair. She lured men with her sultry smile, engaging body language, and silky laugh. In comparison, Gigi considered herself plain, with short, mousy hair and solitary behavior, but she preferred blending in and letting her friend be the center of attention. Gigi rarely ventured beyond her favorite pair of blue jeans, a two-beer night, and watching her friend have all the social action.

"Oh, yes. Hottie at your six," Lexi said. "Don't turn. He'll walk past you."

Gigi glimpsed tight blue jeans below a snug T-shirt as Lexi's potential prey sauntered past their table on the way to the bar. The owner of the clothes leaned on the counter.

"Oh, gross. Gag." Lexi grimaced. "He just stuffed snuff in his lip."

Gigi laughed. "Why would you want to pick up a guy in a bar anyway. Who knows what you're going to get?"

"Would you prefer I look online?"

"I don't endorse that either."

"She says in her no-nonsense, authoritarian police-woman tone," Lexi retorted.

Gigi cracked a smile. "What about at work? You must have some selection of potential suiters at the museum."

"Um. No. Most are taken, and none of the ones left are personable. Besides, the problem with dating someone from work is that if something goes wrong in the relation-ship, I still have to see that person."

"Makes one night stands harder to pull off, too," Gigi teased.

"Exactly." Lexi wriggled her eyebrows.

"Fine. Bar," Gigi grumbled playfully. She wouldn't consider dating anyone she worked with either—not that she was in the market.

The bar had been a happy hunting ground for Lexi so far—if the definition of success was picking up a new man every few months. This wasn't how Gigi judged success, but the pattern seemed to satisfy her friend, who was certainly less lonely, or less *alone*, than Gigi.

Lexi took another drink before tossing her head back and snapping her chocolate curls off her shoulder. "You could live a little."

"Sometimes I want to. It's just this weird ghost thing."

"Which is in the past, right?"

"Clean and sober for five years now. I'm due for my next chip." Gigi raised her beer in a mock toast.

Lexi frowned. "Don't make it sound like a disease."

"It is."

"It's not."

Gigi leaned forward and lowered her voice. "If a person has a condition that completely paralyzes them and causes such profound anxiety that they have to medicate themselves when it happens ... it's a disease."

"You can't shut men out forever just because you used to see ghosts."

"You can't keep letting them all in," Gigi countered with a sassy smirk.

"I live life fully ... no walls, no boundaries."

Gigi didn't point out that her work as a white-collar crime investigator let her see the frailty of life and reinforced her belief in the need for walls and boundaries. Because she wanted to keep their celebratory Thursdays light, she didn't explain how people could be scheming, manipulative, and wholly untrustworthy.

A man approached their table holding a beer in one hand. He wore faded blue jeans and a burgundy collared shirt, and when he spoke, his Irish accent rolled over her, smooth as silk.

"Am I interrupting?"

"Rory, how are you?" Lexi stood with a smile, exchanging a friendly hug before drawing back, one eyebrow arched slightly. "Fancy meeting you here." Her tone suggested the encounter wasn't entirely happenstance.

He smiled back, bright-eyed and charming. "I'm fair. Can I fetch you ladies fresh a pint of gat?"

He turned toward Gigi, giving her a full blast of his boyish smile. She wasn't sure what a gat was, but if Rory and his deep, sensual voice was fetching it for her, she wouldn't turn it down.

Lexi said, "This is my friend, Gigi Montgomery."

Rory extended a hand. "It's a pleasure it is. Lexi has told me about you. You're a detective, right?"

Gigi stood and shook his hand, finding it warm and firm. Rory's eye contact lingered a little longer before he released her, but she didn't mind the long gaze. His strong, cleanly shaven jaw and thick, black hair were a sweetly handsome mix, piquing her interest despite her usual reservations.

"Care to join us?" Lexi asked.

"I'd be delighted, if I'm not intruding."

"Not at all."

"How do you two know each other?" Gigi asked, wondering if this gorgeous man with long, dark lashes would turn into Lexi's date for the night.

"Through the museum," Lexi began, "Rory—"

"Is helping with one of the displays," he interrupted.

Lexi regarded him for a moment but only smiled when Gigi frowned at their odd behavior.

"You're out of your Guinness. Can I get you another?" He gestured toward Gigi's beer.

"Yes, thanks."

He stood back up and walked to the bar.

Gigi turned toward Lexi with her mouth agape. "You work with him?"

"Yeah. He's uh … helping."

Gigi eyed her friend, unsure why her behavior had turned cagey around Rory. Did she like him? She'd never mentioned him.

"Are you dating him?" Gigi asked.

Lexi choked on her beer. "No. No, definitely not. No fraternizing with co-workers, remember?"

Before Gigi could dig deeper into Lexi's odd reply, Rory reappeared.

Gigi thanked him for the drink. "Lexi tells me you're helping at the museum. What exhibit?"

"An array of Irish artifacts. Some from Cathal mac Figuine."

"He was a king, right?"

Rory arched an eyebrow—a motion Gigi decided should be illegal for a man as attractive as him. "*Sea*, king of Munster, Southern Ireland. You know Irish history?"

"Only a little."

"Gigi solved the mystery of a stolen plate from the Irish display at the Art Institute of Chicago," Lexi said.

Gigi swallowed a sip of her beer. "I learned a little Irish history in the process. I'd love to see the exhibit you're working on." She looked back and forth from Lexi to Rory to make it clear she was asking the both of them. She would never make a play on someone Lexi might be interested in dating—assuming she knew how to make a play, because dating wasn't something she'd had much experience initiating.

Rory nodded, brown eyes looking only at her and somehow making her feel she was the only person there. "It's not open yet, but we could go opening night, which is in three days' time."

"That sounds great." Gigi smiled, feeling oddly like this man's presence cast some sort of spell over her. Normally cautious and conservative, she was agreeing to an invitation that felt like a date. Perhaps she was reading too much into the man's magnetism.

They were interrupted when a tall, tan blonde woman strode up to their table. She wore jeans and a puffy white jacket with her hands fisted inside the pockets. A man with a long scruffy beard in tattered blue jeans trailed behind her.

"I heard you were back in the states." The woman addressed Rory in a cold, bitter tone.

"Hello, Ilene. It's been a while. Is this your new *ghrá*?" Rory's voice became deep and flat, nothing like the friendly tone Gigi had just heard when talking of Ireland antiques.

"Yes."

"So, it's official then?"

"I told you it was," Ilene snapped.

"No, you *texted* it was over, which wasn't adult behavior."

She put one hand on her hip. "Well, you dragged me to this dump, so now it's in person."

"So, it is." He kept his voice the same even tone.

"Where's my stuff, Rory?"

He withdrew a key from his pocket and handed it to Ilene.

"What is this?" she demanded.

"The key to a storage facility." He pulled a business card out of his pocket and offered it to her. "This storage facility."

"You put my things in storage?" Her tone was thick with incredulous shock.

"You were gone for eight months. I'd not a word for six of them."

"I texted."

"Like I said, not a word."

Ilene scoffed as she snatched the card out of his hand and spun toward the exit. She stormed out with the homeless looking man on her heels.

Lexi turned to Rory with a grimace. "That looked rather officially over. Didn't sound like there was much actual dating."

Rory—jaw firm and eyes narrowed—turned away from Ilene and back to Lexi. He nodded before scowling down at his beer.

"Oh. Handsome man at the bar just gave me the chin nod." Lexi stood, her attention derailed like a squirrel after a nut. "I *must* explore this further."

Gigi shoved to her feet and grabbed Lexi by the elbow. "Girls' night, remember?" She kept her voice to a harsh whisper as she glanced back at Rory who seemed to be studying the condensation on his bottle. "You're not leaving me here."

"Now's your chance. Rory's single." Lexi winked.

Gigi looked at her friend with a horrified expression. "His girlfriend just broke up with him. I'm not hitting on him now."

"This may have been the official break up, but it's obviously been over for a while."

Lexi pulled away, and Gigi was forced to turn around and acknowledge she was alone with a tall, handsome, and newly single man.

"Are you okay?" she asked lamely as she sat back down, wrapping her hands around her beer.

He ran a hand through his dark, wavy hair. "Sorry for the public ructions. I knew the end was coming. It had already happened, actually. I wanted to force her to look me in the eye and act like an adult."

"Well, she looked you in the eye."

He chuckled. "Yeah, I guess I accomplished one thing. I'm more upset I ever dated her in the first place than that it's over. I made bags of it. I should've just let it go months past when she texted me." He slowly turned his glass of beer on the table in a circle with long, dexterous fingers.

"Made bags of it?" she asked.

"It's an Irish phrase, meaning I handled it wrong."

"From my viewpoint, she's the one who made bags of it. Letting you go was an idiotic move on her part. And really? That other guy instead?"

"Apparently she went on a medical mission trip and found her true love."

"Her loss," Gigi said, holding up her glass for a toast.

The corner of his mouth turned up.

> *"Always remember to forget*
> *the things that made you sad.*
> *But never forget to remember*
> *the things that made you glad."*

He clinked his glass to hers.

"I like that toast," she said.

He swallowed a sip and tossed out another,

> *"To a long life and a joyful one.*
> *Good health and a happy one.*
> *A cold pint–and another one!"*

She laughed, and they toasted again.

"In my country, we've quite an array of toasts," he said.

"Okay, my turn, Irishman.

> *May the winds of fortune lift your sail.*
> *May you navigate a gentle sea.*
> *May it always be the other man*
> *who says, 'this drink's on me.'"*

"Well done, Detective." He accepted the toast with an adorable lopsided grin that made her heart flutter.

Lexi appeared and looked back and forth between Rory

and Gigi. "You're okay? I'm heading out with the snuff dipper."

"Seriously?" Gigi cringed.

Lexi shrugged. "Kissing is optional."

"Text me later!" she called as Lexi exited the bar with the man.

"She always leaves with someone." Gigi turned back to Rory, shaking her head in part amazement, part disbelief.

Rory arched his eyebrows. "And do you?"

"I have higher standards." That was definitely the reason. It was most certainly not because she feared rejection when someone found out her affliction. Or that most men were intimidated by her being a cop.

Rory nodded but remained silent. She felt like she was intruding on his post-break-up reflection time. She didn't know him well enough to offer comfort and needed to squash an absurd urge to take his hand in hers.

"I'm going to call it a night. Thank you for the beer. And the lovely toasts." She stood, but to her surprise he stopped her.

"You haven't eaten dinner, and neither have I. Join me for a bite?"

She considered the offer. Although the prospect of an impromptu date felt awkward, her stomach leaped at the promise of food. She considered her five year no ghosts mark, that she wanted to date again, and how Rory seemed the perfect next step. He was playful, easy on the eyes, and recently single so perhaps unlikely to rush anything serious.

"I'd like that," she said, feeling exhilarated and impulsive for the first time in as long as she could recall.

His phone buzzed. "One second." He looked her directly in the eye as if ensuring she wouldn't think he was dismissing their dinner. "I have to take this, and then we're leaving together." He answered the phone and left the table to go stand in a quieter section of the bar.

She softly strummed her fingers on the wooden tabletop and avoided making eye contact with any of the men seated on stools scanning the room. The difficulty of being a lone woman at a table in a bar was the cyclical offering of men to buy drinks. She faced the same thing every time Lexi abandoned her.

Despite her efforts to look uninterested, a suitor approached. "Can I buy you a drink?" His voice sounded overly heady as he sat in the empty chair across from her.

"I'm waiting for someone," she said.

"You shouldn't drink alone while you're waiting." He was probably her age—around thirty—but had an immaturity about him from the way he slouched in the chair. He set his drink a little too heavily down on the table, an indication it wasn't his first beverage of the night by far.

Gigi pursed her lips. "He's right over there."

The man smiled, but his gaze on her was a little unfocused. "Anyone ever tell you your eyes sparkle like diamonds on the sea?"

"My eyes are green, not blue."

"An emerald sea," he amended.

She silently gave him props for the quick thinking, but still scowled her disinterest at him and the gumption he had to take a seat at her table without asking.

When the uninvited guest didn't move, Gigi reached down and pulled her Chicago PD detective badge out of her blazer pocket. She placed the polished brass in plain view. The drunken suitor's eyes went wide as he began to push away from the table.

"You're a cop." His voice now sounded remarkably sober in contrast to the seductive greasiness a moment ago.

"I'm a cop."

He slunk away from the table just as Rory came back.

The Irishman watched the other man leave before turning a pair of surprised sparkling brown eyes on her. "Was he hitting on you? I'd only stepped aside for two minutes." He sounded amused and impressed.

"He was," Gigi said. She picked up her badge and slipped it back into the inside pocket of her blazer.

"And that worked? You scared him off with your cop badge?"

"It's actually quite effective in eliminating riff-raff."

"As a repellent to suitors?" he asked, disbelief still coloring his voice.

"Only to the ones who have something to hide, or the spineless ones."

Rory laughed—a rich, deep sound Gigi enjoyed. It warmed her from the inside out.

"Well, it won't work on me. You've a noble profession, Detective Montgomery."

"Many men are frightened by the prospect of dating a cop."

"There you're wrong. Boys and cowards may be dissuaded from dating a female cop. Men ... not so much." He offered her his elbow.

Smiling, she stood and accepted it. She couldn't recall

the last time a man escorted her, but Rory walked with her arm in arm from the bar, all the way to the restaurant.

Five years avoiding romance, avoiding ghosts, avoiding anything that made her heart race. And here she was—saying yes to a man whose smile already unraveled her.

<<<~~~CONTINUE READING~~~>>>